'THE BEST OF . . .'
collections are intended to present the
representative stories of the masters of
science fiction in chronological order, their
aim being to provide science fiction readers
with a selection of short stories that
demonstrate the authors' literary
development and at the same time providing
new readers with a sound introduction to
their work.

The collections were compiled with the help
and advice of the authors concerned,
together with the invaluable assistance of
numerous fans, without whose good work,
time and patience they would not have been
published.

In particular the advice of Roger Peyton,
Gerald Bishop, Peter Weston and Leslie
Flood is appreciated.

ANGUS WELLS, *Editor*, 1973

The Best of Arthur C. Clarke

SPHERE BOOKS LIMITED
30/32 Gray's Inn Road, London WC1X 8JL

First published in Great Britain by Sphere Books Ltd 1973
Reprinted 1975
Copyright © Arthur C. Clarke 1973
Anthology copyright © Sphere Books Ltd 1973
Introduction copyright © Arthur C. Clarke 1973
Bibliography copyright © Gerald Bishop 1973
This edition reprinted 1976 originally published in one
volume entitled The Best of Arthur C. Clarke.

TRADE
MARK

Set in Linotype Times

Printed in Great Britain by
Hazell Watson & Viney Ltd
Aylesbury, Bucks

CONTENTS

ACKNOWLEDGMENTS

Travel by Wire: *Amateur Science Stories*, 1937
Retreat from Earth: *Amateur Science Stories*, 1938
The Awakening: *Zenith*, 1942
Whacky: *Fantasy*, 1942
Castaway: *Fantasy*, 1947
History Lesson: *Startling Stories*, 1949
Hide and Seek: *Astounding Science Fiction*, 1949
Second Dawn: *Science Fiction Quarterly*, 1951
The Sentinel: *Ten Story Fantasy*, 1951
The Star: *Infinity Science Fiction*, 1955
Refugee: *Fantasy*, 1955

1933: A SCIENCE-FICTION ODYSSEY

by

ARTHUR C. CLARKE

WHAT makes a writer tick? One element in his composition is certainly the desire to show off. The earliest memory of my schooldays is of standing in front of the class and spinning stories about prehistoric animals. In this I must have been encouraged by the village schoolmaster, Mr. Tipper. I have been lucky with my teachers; though some were better than others, I do not remember a bad one.

When I was about nine (on the other side of the Atlantic, Goddard had just launched his first liquid-fuelled rocket ...) Mr. Tipper felt that I needed wider academic horizons than could be provided by Bishops Lydeard, population *circa* 500. So I was transferred to Huish's Grammar School, Taunton, where I received my secondary education and remained until I entered the Civil Service in 1936 at the age of nineteen.

At Huish, under the influence of the English master Captain E. B. Mitford, I began to write sketches and short stories for the School Magazine. A third of a century later I was able to repay something of my debt by dedicating 'The Nine Billion Names of God' to 'Mitty, my first editor'.

I can still recall those editorial sessions back in the early 1930s. About once a week, after class, Mitty would gather his schoolboy staff together, and we would all sit around a table on which there was a large bag of toffees. Bright ideas were rewarded instantly; Mitty invented positive reinforcement years before B. F. Skinner. He also employed a heavy metre rule for *negative* reinforcement, but this was used only in class – never, so far as I recall, at editorial conferences.

My first printed words thus appeared in the *Huish Maga-*

zine, where I eventually published at least a dozen items, totalling several thousand words. Most of these pieces were only of ephemeral interest, being full of topical allusions which not even the author can now identify. However, even in those days my science-fictional tendencies were obvious, as will be seen from the following letter from 'Ex-Sixth Former' stationed at a torrid and high-altitude Outpost of Empire: Vrying Pan, British Malaria.

It is almost impossible to keep any liquid except under enormous pressure. However, with the powerful refrigerating plant at the rubber mines here it is possible to reduce water to its boiling point, which is a great convenience to us in the hot weather.

The precautions we have to take to preserve our lives are extraordinary. Our houses are built on the principle of the Dewar vacuum flask, to keep out the heat, and the outsides are silvered to reflect the sunlight ... We have to take great care to avoid cutting ourselves in any way, for if this happens our blood soon boils and evaporates.

Electricity is very cheap here, as we can get large supplies from thermocouples. The hot end is in the sun, and the cold terminal in the boiler room at the mines, which is the coolest place in Vrying Pan ...

However, I must leave off now as my ink has evaporated, in spite of the water-cooled jacket of my fountain pen.

This effort graced the Xmas 1933 issue of the *Huish Magazine* – which, for good measure, also contains two other short pieces, heavily disguised under the pseudonym 'Clericus'. They must mark my first appearance in print.

Even in 1933, I was obviously already writing about the Moon, and I know why. I had fallen under the spell of the old science-fiction pulps, and can still recall the very first issue I ever owned. The cover of the March 1930 *Astounding Stories of Super Science*, containing Ray Cumming's 'Brigands of the Moon', is still clear and bright in my memory.

During my lunch hour I used to haunt Woolworth's, where issues of *Astounding*, *Amazing* and *Wonder* could be picked up for threepence. Much of the hard-earned money my widowed mother had saved for my food went on these magazines; I regard it as one of the best investments I ever made. I set myself the goal of obtaining a complete set of all the S.F. magazines, and had practically achieved this when the outbreak of war in 1939 caused a slight shift in priorities.

Half a lifetime later, I can still remember the ecstasy of receiving parcels – once even a *crate*! – of S.F. magazines I had bought for a few pence. Eventually I had a collection of three or four hundred magazines, which evaporated some time during the War. It would now be worth a small fortune.

The young readers of today, born into a world where many of the marvels of the 1930s have already come true, and where S.F. magazines, books and films are commonplace instead of rarities that had to be sought like gold, can scarcely imagine the impact of these old pulps. Of course, the literary standards were usually abysmal – but the stories were full of ideas, and amply evoked the famous 'sense of wonder' which is the goal of the best fiction. I see nothing incongruous in applying to those garish magazines Keats' immortal

> *Charmed magic casements, opening on the foam*
> *Of perilous sea, in faery lands forlorn.*

Soon after 1930 I came under the spell of a considerably more literate influence. In the public library at Minehead, the small West of England town where I was born, I discovered a copy of W. Olaf Stapledon's titanic *Last and First*

Men (1930). No book before or since ever had such an impact on me. The Stapledonic vistas of millions and hundreds of millions of years, the rise and fall of civilizations and entire races of men, changed my whole outlook on the universe and has influenced much of my writing ever since.

Twenty years later I was to meet Stapledon, and persuaded him to give a talk entitled 'Interplanetary Man' to the British Interplanetary Society, of which I was then chairman. His was one of the noblest and most civilized spirits I have ever encountered; I am glad that there is now a revival of interest in his work and thought.

But hard-cover books of S.F. were still very rare, and magazines were my mainstay. Through their correspondence columns I made many friends, in particular the English writer Eric Frank Russell, who encouraged my early efforts. It was thanks to Eric that I earned my first cash – as opposed to toffees – from writing. He used one of my ideas in a short story, and paid me handsomely for it. I wish I had kept his long, witty letters, written in the most beautiful hand I have ever seen. In this permissive age, most of them would now be quite printable – but, alas, they too were lost during the war years. Thank you, Eric, for your kindness to an annoyingly persistent schoolboy.

Science fiction has always encouraged an enormous amount of amateur writing, and there have been literally thousands of duplicated (sometimes printed) magazines put out by enthusiastic 'fans'. These have served a very useful purpose in providing launching pads for many professional writers in the field. The first stories I ever completed appeared in some of these magazines, and a few samples may be of interest now. If they do nothing else they may serve as a kind of absolute zero from which my later writing may be calibrated.

'The Awakening' appeared in the February 1942 issue

(No. 4) of *Zenith*, edited in Manchester by Harry Turner and Marion Eadie. A revised version was published in *Reach for Tomorrow*.

'Travel by Wire!' was published in the second issue (December 1937) of *Amateur Science Fiction Stories*, edited in Leeds by Douglas W. F. Mayer. 'Retreat From Earth' appeared in the third (and last!) issue, dated March 1938 – which also contained another story of mine, 'How We Went to Mars'.

'Whacky' appeared in *Fantast*, edited by Douglas Webster of Aberdeen, of July 1942 (Vol. 3, No. 2, whole number 14). The same issue contains my first serial, of interest only to S.F. fans: 'A Short History of Fantocracy'. I am happy to see how many of the characters therein are still active, thirty years later.

Incidentally, I have discovered with much interest that some of these ancient magazines contain perfectly dreadful pieces by a certain Ray Bradbury. I am keeping them carefully for purposes of blackmail.

Just before the War, the first British S.F. Magazine *Tales of Wonder* was put together by Walter H. Gillings. Walter did more than buy my first articles and stories – he *gave* me my first typewriter, which I carried home on a London bus from his home in Ilford. And he is the only editor I ever encountered who turned a story down, saying that it was too good for him – and a rival editor would pay more. The least I could do in gratitude was to dedicate my first collection, *Expedition to Earth*, to him.

But in spite of the traditions of Wells, Doyle, Haggard and Kipling, S.F. did not flourish in England and its spiritual home was still the United States – as in many ways it still is. I sold my first stories to John Campbell of *Astounding* (later *Analog*) during the closing months of the War, while I was in the Royal Air Force. His first purchase was 'Rescue Party' – though 'Loophole', sold a little later,

13

actually appeared first. At the time of these sales (1945) I was stationed just outside Stratford-on-Avon, and I remember thinking modestly that there was something singularly appropriate about this.

The stories that follow were written, therefore, during a period of thirty years from 1933 to 1963. They were selected by Sphere's editor Angus Wells from my six volumes of short stories, which contain virtually everything I have written in this genre.

These tales should speak for themselves and I do not think it is appropriate to comment further on them. However, there is an historical footnote to 'Death and the Senator' which is of some interest. This story was written in 1961, long before the great days of the U.S. space programme, and foretold an era when it had fallen on hard times – as has indeed happened. And now Nature has imitated Art, for this fictional account of a U.S. space committee hearing has *itself* been read as evidence to the House of Representatives Committee on Astronautics (March 14th, 1972)! I hasten to add that though I have known all the NASA Administrators, none of them is reflected in the character of Dr. Harkness.

And I suppose everyone knows what happened to 'The Sentinel', sixteen years after I wrote it at Christmas 1948. Those who would like detailed instructions for turning a 'glittering pyramid' into a black monolith will find them in *The Lost Worlds of 2001.*

ARTHUR C. CLARKE

Colombo, Sri Lanka
December 1972

Amateur Science Fiction Stories: December, 1937: vol. 1 no. 2

TRAVEL BY WIRE!

You people can have no idea of the troubles and trials we had to endure before we perfected the radio-transporter, not that it's quite perfect even yet. The greatest difficulty, as it had been in television thirty years before, was improving definition, and we spent nearly five years over that little problem. As you will have seen in the Science Museum, the first object we transmitted was a wooden cube, which was assembled all right, only instead of being one solid block it consisted of millions of little spheres. In fact, it looked just like a solid edition of one of the early television pictures, for instead of dealing with the object molecule by molecule or better still electron by electron, our scanners took little chunks at a time.

This didn't matter for some things, but if we wanted to transmit objects of art, let alone human beings, we would have to improve the process considerably. This we managed to do by using the delta-ray scanners all round our subject, above, below, right, left, in front and behind. It was a lovely game synchronizing all six, I can tell you, but when it was done we found that the transmitted elements were ultra-microscopic in size, which was quite good enough for most purposes.

Then, when they weren't looking, we borrowed a guinea pig from the biology people on the 37th floor, and sent it through the apparatus. It came through in excellent condition, except for the fact it was dead. So we had to return it to its owner with a polite request for a post-mortem. They raved a bit at first, saying that the unfortunate creature had been inoculated with the only specimens of some germs

15

they'd spent months rearing from the bottle. They were so annoyed, in fact, that they flatly refused our request.

Such insubordination on the part of mere biologists was of course deplorable, and we promptly generated a high-frequency field in their laboratory and gave them all fever for a few minutes. The post-mortem results came up in half an hour, the verdict being that the creature was in perfect condition but had died of shock, with a rider to the effect that if we wanted to try the experiment again we should blindfold our victims. We were also told that a combination lock had been fitted to the 37th floor to protect it from the depredations of kleptomaniacal mechanics who should be washing cars in a garage. We could not let this pass, so we immediately X-rayed their lock and to their complete consternation told them what the key-word was.

That is the best of being in our line, you can always do what you like with the other people. The chemists on the next floor were our only serious rivals, but we generally came out on top. Yes, I remember that time they slipped some vile organic stuff into our lab. through a hole in the ceiling. We had to work in respirators for a month, but we had our revenge later. Every night after the staff had left, we used to send a dose of mild cosmics into the lab. and curdled all their beautiful precipitates, until one evening old Professor Hudson stayed behind and we nearly finished him off. But to get back to my story —

We obtained another guinea pig, chloroformed it, and sent it through the transmitter. To our delight, it revived. We immediately had it killed and stuffed for the benefit of posterity. You can see it in the museum with the rest of our apparatus.

But if we wanted to start a passenger service, this would never do – it would be too much like an operation to suit most people. However, by cutting down the transmitting time to a ten-thousandth of a second, and thus reducing the shock, we managed to send another guinea pig in full possession of its faculties. This one was also stuffed.

The time had obviously come for one of us to try out the apparatus but as we realized what a loss it would be to humanity should anything go wrong, we found a suitable victim in the person of Professor Kingston, who teaches Greek or something foolish on the 197th floor. We lured him to the transmitter with a copy of *Homer*, switched on the field, and by the row from the receiver, we knew he'd arrived safely and in full possession of his faculties, such as they were. We would have liked to have had him stuffed as well, but it couldn't be arranged.

After that we went through in turns, found the experience quite painless, and decided to put the device on the market. I expect you can remember the excitement there was when we first demonstrated our little toy to the Press. Of course we had the dickens of a job convincing them that it wasn't a fake, and they didn't really believe it until they had been through the transporter themselves. We drew the line, though, at Lord Rosscastle, who would have blown the fuses even if we could have got him into the transmitter.

This demonstration gave us so much publicity that we had no trouble at all in forming a company. We bade a reluctant farewell to the Research Foundation, told the remaining scientists that perhaps one day we'd heap coals of fire on their heads by sending them a few millions, and started to design our first commercial senders and receivers.

The first service was inaugurated on May 10th, 1962. The ceremony took place in London, at the transmitting end, though at the Paris receiver there were enormous crowds watching to see the first passengers arrive, and probably hoping they wouldn't. Amid cheers from the assembled thousands, the Prime Minister pressed a button (which wasn't connected to anything), the chief engineer threw a switch (which was) and a large Union Jack faded from view and appeared again in Paris, rather to the annoyance of some patriotic Frenchmen.

After that, passengers began to stream through at a rate which left the Customs officials helpless. The service was a great and instantaneous success, as we only charged £2 per person. This we considered very moderate, for the electricity used cost quite one-hundredth of a penny.

Before long we had services to all the big cities of Europe, by cable that is, not radio. A wired system was safer, though it was dreadfully difficult to lay polyaxial cables, costing £500 a mile, under the Channel. Then, in conjunction with the Post Office, we began to develop internal services between the large towns. You may remember our slogans 'Travel by Phone' and 'It's quicker by Wire' which were heard everywhere in 1963. Soon, practically everyone used our circuits and we were handling thousands of tons of freight per day.

Naturally, there were accidents, but we could point out that we had done what no Minister of Transport had ever done, reduced road fatalities to a mere ten thousand a year. We lost one client in six million, which was pretty good even to start with, though our record is even better now. Some of the mishaps that occurred were very peculiar indeed, and in fact there are quite a few cases which we haven't explained to the dependents yet, or to the insurance companies either.

One common complaint was earthing along the line. When that happened, our unfortunate passenger was just dissipated into nothingness. I suppose his or her molecules would be distributed more or less evenly over the entire earth. I remember one particularly gruesome accident when the apparatus failed in the middle of a transmission. You can guess the result ... Perhaps even worse was what happened when two lines got crossed and the currents were mixed.

18

Of course, not all accidents were as bad as these. Sometimes, owing to a high resistance in the circuit, a passenger would lose anything up to five stone in transit, which generally cost us about £1000 and enough free meals to restore the missing enbonpoint. Fortunately, we were soon able to make money out of this affair, for fat people came along to be reduced to manageable dimensions. We made a special apparatus which transmitted massive dowagers round resistance coils and reassembled them where they started, minus the cause of the trouble. '*So* quick, my dear, and *quite* painless! I'm *sure* they could take off that 150 pounds you want to lose in no time! Or is it 200?'

We also had a good deal of trouble through interference and induction. You see, our apparatus picked up various electrical disturbances and superimposed them on the object under transmission. As a result many people came out looking like nothing on earth and very little on Mars or Venus. They could usually be straightened out by the plastic surgeons, but some of the products had to be seen to be believed.

Fortunately these difficulties have been largely overcome now that we use the micro-beams for our carrier, though now and then accidents still occur. I expect you remember that big lawsuit we had last year with Lita Cordova, the television star, who claimed £1,000,000 damages from us for alleged loss of beauty. She asserted that one of her eyes had moved during a transmission, but I couldn't see any difference myself and nor could the jury, who had enough opportunity. She had hysterics in the court when our Chief Electrician went into the box and said bluntly, to the alarm of both side's lawyers, that if anything really *had* gone wrong with the transmission, Miss Cordova wouldn't have been able to recognize herself had any cruel person handed her a mirror.

Lots of people ask us when we'll have a service to Venus

19

or Mars. Doubtless that will come in time, but of course the difficulties are pretty considerable. There is so much sun static in space, not to mention the various reflecting layers everywhere. Even the micro-waves are stopped by the Appleton 'Q' layer at 100,000 km, you know. Until we can pierce that, Interplanetary shares are still safe.

Well, I see it's nearly 22, so I'd best be leaving. I have to be in New York by midnight. What's that? Oh no, I'm going by plane. *I* don't travel by wire! You see, I helped invent the thing!

Rockets for me! Good night!

Amateur Science Fiction Stories: March, 1938: vol. 1 no. 3

RETREAT FROM EARTH

A GREAT many millions of years ago, when man was a dream of the distant future, the third ship to reach Earth in all history descended through the perpetual clouds on to what is now Africa, and the creatures it had carried across an unthinkable abyss of space looked out upon a world which would be a fit home for their weary race. But Earth was already inhabited by a great though dying people, and since both races were civilized in the true sense of the word, they did not go to war but made a mutual agreement. For those who then ruled Earth had once ruled everywhere within the orbit of Pluto, had planned always for the future and even at their end they had prepared Earth for the race that was to come after them.

So, forty million years after the last of the old ones had gone to his eternal rest, men began to rear their cities where once the architects of a greater race had flung their towers against the clouds. And in the long echoing centuries before the birth of man, the aliens had not been idle but had covered half the planet with their cities, filled with blind, fantastic slaves, and though man knew these cities, for they often caused him infinite trouble, yet he never suspected that all around him in the tropics an older civilization than his was planning busily for the day when it would once again venture forth upon the seas of space to regain its lost inheritance.

'Gentlemen,' said the President of the Council gravely, 'I am sorry to say that we have received a severe setback in our plans to colonize the third planet. As you all know, we have for many years been working on that planet unknown to its inhabitants, preparing for the day when we should take over complete control. We anticipated no resistance, for the people of Three are at a very primitive level of development, and possess no weapons which could harm us. Moreover, they are continually quarrelling among themselves owing to the extraordinary number of political groups or "nations" into which they are divided, a lack of unity which will no doubt be a considerable help to our plans.

'To obtain the fullest possible knowledge of the planet and its peoples, we have had several hundred investigators working on Three, a number in each important city. Our men have done very well, and thanks to their regular reports we now have a detailed knowledge of this strange world. In fact, until a few setas ago I would have said that we knew everything of importance concerning it, but now I find that we were very much mistaken.

'Our chief investigator in the country known as England, which has been mentioned here on a number of occasions, was that very intelligent young student, Cervac Theton, grandson of the great Vorac. He progressed splendidly with the English, a particularly guileless race it seems, and was soon accepted into their highest society. He even spent some time at one of their great seats of learning (so called) but soon left in disgust. Though it had nothing to do with his real purpose, this energetic young man also studied the wild animals of Three, for remarkable though it seems there are a great many strange and interesting creatures roaming freely over large areas of the planet. Some are actually dangerous to man, but he has conquered most of them and even exterminated some species. It was while studying these beasts that Cervac made the discovery which I fear may change our whole plan of action. But let Cervac speak for himself.'

The President threw a switch, and from concealed speakers Cervac Theton's voice rang out over that assembly of the greatest brains of Mars.

'– come to what is the most important part of this communication. For some time I have been studying the many wild creatures of this planet, purely for the sake of scientific knowledge. The animals of Three are divided into four main groups – mammals, fishes, reptiles and insects, and a number of lesser groups. There have been many representatives of the first three classes on our own planet, though of course there are none now, but as far as I know there have never been insects on our world at any time in its history. Consequently they attracted my attention from the first, and I made a careful study of their habits and structure.

'You who have never seen them will have great difficulty in imagining what these creatures are like. There are millions of different types, and it would take ages to classify all of them, but they are mostly small animals with many jointed limbs and with a hard armoured body. They are usually very small, about half a zem in length, and are often winged. Most of them lay eggs and undergo a number of metamorphoses before they become perfect creatures. I am sending with this report a number of photographs and films which will give you a better idea of their infinite variety than any words of mine. I obtained most of my information on the subject from the literature which has been built up by thousands of patient students who have devoted their lives to watching insects at work. The inhabitants of Three have taken much interest in the creatures which share their world, and this, I think, is another proof that they are more intelligent than some of our scientists would have us believe.'

At this there were smiles in the audience, for the House of Theton had always been noted for its radical and unorthodox views.

'In my studies I came across accounts of some extraordinary creatures which live in the tropical regions of the planet. They are called "termites" or "white ants" and live

23

in large, wonderfully organized communities. They even have cities – huge mounds, honey-combed with passages and made of exceedingly hard materials. They can perform prodigious feats of engineering, being able to bore through metals and glass, and they can destroy most of man's creations when they wish. They eat cellulose, that is, wood, and since man uses this material extensively he is always waging war on these destroyers of his possessions. Perhaps luckily for him, the termites have even deadlier enemies, the ants, which are a very similar type of creature. These two races have been at war for geological ages, and the outcome is still undecided.

'Although they are blind, the termites cannot endure light and so even when they venture from their cities they always keep under cover, making tunnels and cement tubes if they have to cross open country. They are wonderful engineers and architects and no ordinary obstacle will deflect them from their purpose. Their most remarkable achievement, however, is a biological one. From the same eggs they can produce half a dozen different types of specialized creature. Thus they can breed fighters with immense claws, soldiers which can spray poison over their opponents, workers which act as food stores by virtue of their immense distended stomachs and a number of other fantastic mutations. You will find a full account of them, as far as they are known to the naturalists of Three, in the books I am sending.

'The more I read of their achievements, the more I was impressed by the perfection of their social system. It occurred to me, as indeed it had to many previous students, that a termitary may be compared to a vast machine, whose component parts are not of metal but of protoplasm, whose wheels and cogs are separate insects, each with some pre-ordained role to perform. It was not until later that I found how near the truth this analogy was.

'Nowhere in the termitary is there any waste or disorder,

24

and everywhere there is mystery. As I considered the matter it seemed to me that the termites were much more worthy of our attention, from the purely scientific point of view, than man himself. After all, man is not so very different from ourselves, though I shall annoy many by saying so, yet these insects are utterly alien to us in every way. They work, live and die for the good of the state. To them the individual is nothing. With us, and with man, the state exists only for the individual. Who shall say which is right?

'These problems so engrossed me that I eventually decided to study the little creatures myself with all the instruments at my command, instruments of which the naturalists of Three had never dreamt. So I selected a small uninhabited island in a lonely part of the Pacific, the greatest ocean of Three, where the strange mounds of the termites clustered thickly, and constructed on it a little metal building to serve as a laboratory. As I was thoroughly impressed by the creatures' destructive powers, I cut a wide circular moat round the building, leaving enough room for my ship to land, and let the sea flow in. I thought that ten zets of water would keep them from doing any mischief. How foolish that moat looks now.

'These preparations took several weeks for it was not very often that I was able to leave England. In my little space-yacht the journey from London to Termite Island took under half a sector so little time was lost in this way. The laboratory was equipped with everything I considered might be useful and many things for which I could see no conceivable use, but which might possibly be required. The most important instrument was a high-powered gamma-ray televisor which I hoped would reveal to me all the secrets hidden from ordinary sight by the walls of the termitary. Perhaps equally useful was a very sensitive psychometer, of the kind we use when exploring planets on which new types of mentalities may exist, and which we might not detect in the ordinary way. The device could operate on any conceivable mind frequency, and at its highest amplification could locate a man several hundred miles away. I was certain that even if the termites possessed only the faintest glimmers of an utterly alien intelligence, I would be able to detect their mental processes.

'At first I made relatively little progress. With the televisor I examined all the nearest termitaries, and fascinating work it was following the workers along the passages of their homes as they carried food and building materials hither and thither. I watched the enormous bloated queen in the royal nursery, laying her endless stream of eggs, one every few seconds, night and day, year after year. Although she was the centre of the colony's activities, yet when I focused the psychometer on her the needles did not so much as flicker. The very cells of my body could do better than that! The monstrous queen was only a brainless mechanism, none the less mechanical because she was made of protoplasm, and the workers looked after her with the care we would devote to one of our useful robots.

'For a number of reasons I had not expected the queen to be the ruling force of the colony, but when I began to explore with psychometer and televisor, nowhere could I discover any creature, any super-termite, which directed and supervised the operations of the rest. This would not have surprised the scientists of Three, for they hold that the termites are governed by instinct alone. But my instrument could have detected the nervous stimuli which constitute automatic reflex actions, and yet I found nothing. I would turn up the amplification to its utmost, put on a pair of those primitive but very useful "head-phones" and listen hour on hour. Sometimes there would be those faint characteristic cracklings we have never been able to explain, but generally the only sound was the subdued washing noise, like waves breaking on some far-off beach, caused

26

by the massed intellects of the planet reacting on my apparatus.

'I was beginning to get discouraged when there occurred one of those accidents which happen so often in science. I was dismantling the instrument after another fruitless investigation when I happened to knock the little receiving loop so that it pointed to the ground. To my surprise the needles started flickering violently. By swinging the loop in the usual way I discovered that the exciting source lay almost directly underneath me, though at what distance I could not guess. In the phones was a continuous humming noise, interspersed with sudden flickerings. It sounded for all the world like any electric machine operating, and the frequency, one hundred thousand mega mega cycles, was not one on which minds have ever been known to function before. To my intense annoyance, as you can guess, I had to return to England at once, and so I could not do anything more at the time.

'It was a fortnight before I could return to Termite Island, and in that time I had to overhaul my little space-yacht owing to an electrical fault. At some time in her history, which I know to have been an eventful one, she had been fitted with ray screens. They were, moreover, very good ray screens, much too good for a law-abiding ship to possess. I have every reason to believe, in fact, that more than once they have defied the cruisers of the Assembly. I did not much relish the task of checking over the complex automatic relay circuits, but at last it was done and I set off at top speed for the Pacific, travelling so fast that my bow wave must have been one continuous explosion. Unfortunately, I soon had to slow down again, for I found that the directional beam I had installed on the island was no longer functioning. I presumed that a fuse had blown, and had to take observations and navigate in the ordinary way. The accident was annoying but not alarming, and I finally spiralled down over Termite Island with no premonition of danger.

'I landed inside my little moat, and went to the door of the laboratory. As I spoke the key-word, the metal seal slid open and a tremendous blast of vapour gushed out of the room. I was nearly stupefied by the stuff, and it was some time before I recovered sufficiently to realize what had happened. When I regained my senses I recognized the smell of hydrogen cyanide, a gas which is instantly fatal to human beings but which only affects us after a considerable time.

'At first I thought that there had been some accident in the laboratory, but I soon remembered that there were not enough chemicals to produce anything like the volume of gas that had gushed out. And in any case, what could possibly have produced such an accident?

'When I turned to the laboratory itself, I had my second shock. One glance was sufficient to show that the place was in ruins. Not a piece of apparatus was recognizable. The cause of the damage was soon apparent – the power plant, my little atomic motor, had exploded. But why? Atomic motors do not explode without very good reason; it would be bad business if they did. I made a careful examination of the room and presently found a number of little holes coming up through the floor – holes such as the termites make when they travel from place to place. My suspicions, incredible though they were, began to be confirmed. It was not completely impossible that the creatures might flood my room with poisonous gas, but to imagine that they understood atomic motors – that was too much! To settle the matter I started hunting for the fragments of the generator, and to my consternation found that the synchronizing coils had been short-circuited. Still clinging to the shattered remnants of the osmium toroid were the jaws of the termite that had been sacrificed to wreck the motor ...

28

'For a long time I sat in the ship, considering these outstanding facts. Obviously, the damage had been wrought by the intelligence I had located for a moment on my last visit. If it were the termite ruler, and there was nothing else it could very well be, how did it come to possess its knowledge of atomic motors and the only way in which to wreck them? For some reason, possibly because I was prying too deeply into its secrets, it had decided to destroy me and my works. Its first attempt had been unsuccessful, but it might try again with better results, though I did not imagine that it could harm me inside the stout walls of my yacht.

'Although my psychometer and televisor had been destroyed, I was determined not to be defeated so easily, and started hunting with the ship's televisor, which though not made for this kind of work could do it very well. Since I lacked the essential psychometer it was some time before I found what I was looking for. I had to explore great sections of the ground with my instrument, focusing the view point through stratum after stratum and examining any suspicious rock that came into the field. When I was at a depth of nearly two hundred feet, I noticed a dark mass looming faintly in the distance, rather like a very large boulder embedded in the soil. But when I approached I saw with a great feeling of elation that it was no boulder, but a perfect sphere of metal, about twenty feet in diameter. My search had ended. There was a slight fading of the image as I drove the beam through the metal, and then on the screen lay revealed the lair of the super-termite.

'I had expected to find some fantastic creature, perhaps a great naked brain with vestigal limbs, but at a glance I could see that there was no living thing in that sphere. From wall to wall that metal-enclosed space was packed with a maze of machinery, most of it very minute and almost unthinkably complex, and all of it clicking and buzzing with lightning-like rapidity. Compared to this miracle of electrical

29

engineering, our great television exchanges would seem the creations of children or savages. I could see myriads of tiny relays operating, director valves flashing intermittantly, and strangely shaped cams spinning among moving mazes of apparatus utterly unlike anything we have ever built. To the makers of this machinery, my atomic generator must have seemed a toy.

'For perhaps two seconds I gazed in wonder at that amazing sight, and then, suddenly and incredibly, an obliterating veil of interference slashed down and the screen was a dancing riot of formless colour.

'Here was something we have never been able to produce – a screen which the televisor could not penetrate. The power of this strange creature was even greater than I had imagined, and in the face of this latest revelation I no longer felt safe even in my ship. In fact, I had a sudden desire to put as many miles as possible between myself and Termite Island. This impulse was so strong that a minute later I was high over the Pacific, rising up through the stratosphere in the great ellipse which would curve down again in England.

'Yes, you may smile or accuse me of cowardice, saying that my grandfather Vorac would not have done so – but listen.

'I was about a hundred miles from the island, thirty miles high and already travelling at two thousand miles an hour when there came a sudden crashing of relays, and the low purr of the motors changed to a tremendous deep-throated roar as an overload was thrown on to them. A glance at the board showed me what had happened – the ray screens were on, flaring beneath the impact of a heavy induction beam. But there was comparatively little power behind the beam, though had I been nearer it would have been a very different tale, and my screens dissipated it without much trouble. Nevertheless, the occurrence gave me an unpleasant shock for the moment, until I remembered that old trick of electrical warfare and threw the full field of my geodesic generators into the beam. I switched on the televisor just in time to see the incandescent fragments of Termite Island fall back into the Pacific ...

'So I returned to England, with one problem solved and a dozen greater ones formulated. How was it that the Termite-brain, as I supposed the machine to be, had never revealed itself to humans? They have often destroyed the homes of its peoples, but as far as I know it has never retaliated. Yet directly I appeared it attacked me, though I was doing it no harm! Perhaps, by some obscure means, it knew that I was not a man, but an adversary worthy of its powers. Or perhaps, though I do not put the suggestion seriously, it is a kind of guardian protecting Three from invaders such as ourselves.

'Somewhere there is an inconsistency that I cannot understand. On the one hand we have that incredible intelligence possessing much, if not all of our knowledge, while on the other are the blind, relatively helpless insects waging an endless war with puny weapons against enemies their ruler could exterminate instantly and without effort. Behind this mad system there must be a purpose, but it is beyond my comprehension. The only rational explanation I can conceive is that for most of the time the termite brain is content to let its subjects go their own, mechanical ways, and that only very seldom, perhaps once in an age, does it take an active part in guiding them. As long as it is not seriously interfered with, it is content to let man do what he likes. It may even take a benevolent interest in him and his works.

'Fortunately for us, the super-termite is not invulnerable. Twice it miscalculated in its dealings with me, and the second time cost it its existence – I cannot say life. I am confident that we can overcome the creature, for it, or others like it, still control the remaining billions of the race.

I have just returned from Africa, and termites there are still organized as they have always been. On this excursion I did not leave my ship, or even land. I believe I have incurred the enmity of an entire race and I am taking no chances. Until I have an armoured cruiser and a staff of expert biologists, I am leaving the termites strictly alone. Even then I shall not feel quite safe, for there may be yet more powerful intelligences on Three than the one I encountered. That is a risk we must take, for unless we can defeat these beings, Planet Three will never be safe for our kind.'

The President cut off the record and turned to the waiting assembly.

'You have heard Theton's report,' he said, 'I appreciate its importance and at once sent a heavy cruiser to Three. As soon as it arrived, Theton boarded it and left for the Pacific.

'That was two days ago. Since then I have heard from neither Theton nor the cruiser, but I do know this:

'An hour after the ship left England, we picked up the radiations from her screens, and in a very few seconds other disturbances – cosmics, ultra-cosmics, induction and tremendous long-wave, low quantum radiations such as we have never used in battle – began to come through in ever-increasing quantities. This lasted for nearly three minutes, when suddenly there came one titanic blast of energy, lasting for a fraction of a second and then – nothing. That final burst of power could have been caused by nothing less than the detonation of an entire atomic generating plant, and must have jarred Three to its core.

'I have called this meeting to put the facts of the matter before you and to ask you to vote on the subject. Shall we abandon our plans for Three, or shall we send one of our most powerful super-dreadnoughts to the planet? One ship could do as much as an entire section of the Fleet in this matter, and would be safe, in case ... but I cannot imagine any power which could defeat such a ship as our "Zuranther". Will you please register your votes in the usual way? It will be a great setback if we cannot colonize Three, but it is not the only planet in the system, though it is the fairest.'

There came subdued clicks and a faint humming of motors as the councillors pressed their coloured buttons, and on the television screen appeared the words: For 967; Against 233.

'Very well, the "Zuranther" will leave at once for Three. This time we will follow her movements with the televisor and then if anything does go wrong, we shall at least obtain some idea of the weapons the enemy uses.'

Hours later the tremendous mass of the flagship of the Martian fleet dropped thunderously through the outer reaches of Earth's atmosphere towards the far-off waters of the Pacific. She fell in the heart of a tornado, for her captain was taking no chances and the winds of the stratosphere were being annihilated by her flaming ray screens.

But on a tiny island far over the eastern horizon, the termites had been preparing for the attack they knew must come, and strange, fragile mechanisms had been erected by myriad blind and toiling insects. The great Martian warship was two hundred miles away when her captain located the island in his televisor. His finger reached towards the button which would start the enormous ray generators, but swift as he was the almost instant acting relays of the termite mind were far swifter. Though, in any case, the outcome would have been the same.

The great spherical screens did not flare even once as the enemy struck home. Their slim rapier of pure heat was driven by only a score of horse-power, while behind the shields of the warship were a thousand million. But the feeble heat beam of the termites never passed through those screens – it reached out through hyperspace to gnaw at the very vitals of the ship. The Martians could not check an enemy who struck from within their defences, an enemy to whom a sphere was no more a barrier than a hollow ring.

The termite rulers, those alien beings from outer space, had kept their agreement with the old lords of earth, and had saved man from the danger his ancestors had long ago foreseen.

But the watching assembly knew only that the screens of the ship which had been blazing fiercely one moment had erupted in a hurricane of flame and a numbing concussion of sound, while for a thousand miles around fragments of white-hot metal were dropping from the heavens.

Slowly the President turned to face the Council and whispered in a low, strained voice, 'I think it had better be planet Two, after all.'

THE AWAKENING

THE Master wondered whether he would dream. That was the only thing he feared, for in a sleep that lasts no more than a night dreams may come that can shatter the mind – and he was to sleep for a hundred years.

He remembered the day, still only a few months ago, when a frightened doctor had said, 'Sir, your heart is failing. You have less than a year to live.' He was not afraid of death, but the thought that it had come upon him in the full flower of his intellect, while his work was still half finished, filled him with a baffled fury. 'And there is nothing you can do?' he asked. 'No, Sir, we have been working on artificial hearts for a hundred years. In another century, perhaps, it might be done.' 'Very well,' he had replied coldly. 'I shall wait another century. You will build me a place where my body will not be disturbed, and then you will put me to sleep by freezing or any other means. That, at least, I know you can do.'

He had watched the building of the tomb, in a secret place above the snow-line of Everest. Only the chosen few must know where the Master was to sleep, for there were many millions in the world who would have sought out his body to destroy it. The secret would be preserved down the generations until the day when man's science had conquered the diseases of the heart. Then the Master would be awakened from his sleep.

He was still conscious when they laid him on the couch in the central chamber, though the drugs had already dimmed his senses. He heard them close the steel doors against their rubber gaskets, and even fancied he could hear the hiss of the pumps which would withdraw the air from around him, and replace it with sterile nitrogen. Then he slept, and in a little while the world forgot the Master.

He slept the hundred years, though rather before that time the discovery he had been awaiting was made. But no one awakened him, for the world had changed since his going and now there were none who would have wished to see him return. His followers had died and mysteriously, the secret of his resting place was lost. For a time the legend of the Master's tomb persisted, but soon it was forgotten. So he slept.

After what by some standards would have been a little while, the earth's crust decided that it had borne the weight of the Himalayas for long enough. Slowly the mountains dropped, tilting the southern plains of India towards the sky. And presently the plateau of Ceylon was the highest point on the surface of the globe, and the ocean above Everest was five and a half miles deep. The Master would not be disturbed by his enemies, or his friends.

Slowly, patiently, the silt drifted down through the towering ocean heights on to the wreck of the Himalayas. The blanket that would some day be chalk began to thicken at the rate of not a few inches every century. If one had returned some time later, one might have found that the sea bed was no longer five miles down, or even four, or three.

Then the land tilted again, and a mighty range of limestone mountains towered where once had been the oceans of Tibet. But the Master knew nothing of this, nor was his sleep disturbed when it happened again ... and again ... and again ...

Now the rain and rivers were washing away the chalk and carrying it out to the new oceans, and the surface was moving down towards the buried tomb. Slowly the miles of rock were washed away, until at last the metal sphere which housed the Master's body returned once more to the light of day – though to a day much longer, and much dimmer, than it had been when the Master closed his eyes. And presently the scientists found him, on a pedestal of rock jutting high above an eroded plain. Because they did not know the secret of the tomb, it took them, for all their wisdom, thirty years to reach the chamber where he slept.

The Master's mind awoke before his body. As he lay powerless, unable even to lift his leaden eyelids, memory came flooding back. The hundred years were safely behind him – his desperate gamble had succeeded! He felt a strange elation, and a longing to see the new world that must have arisen while he lay within his tomb.

One by one, his senses returned. He could feel the hard surface on which he was lying: now a gentle current of air drifted across his brow. Presently he was aware of sounds – faint clickings and scratchings all around him. For a moment he was puzzled: then he realized that the surgeons must be putting their instruments away. He had not yet the strength to open his eyes, so he lay and waited, wondering.

Would men have changed much? Would his name still be remembered among them? Perhaps it would be better if it were not – though he had feared the hatred of neither men nor nations. He had never known their love. Momentarily he wondered if any of his friends might have followed him, but he knew there would be none. When he opened his eyes, all the faces before him would be strange. Yet he longed to see them, to read the expressions they would hold as he awakened from his sleep.

Strength returned. He opened his eyes. The light was gentle, and he was not dazzled, but for a while everything was blurred and misty. He could distinguish figures standing round, but though they seemed strange he could not see them clearly.

Then the Master's eyes came into focus, and as they brought their message to his mind he screamed once, feebly, and died for ever. For in the last moment of his life, as he saw what stood around him, he knew that the long war between Man and Insect was ended – and that Man was not the victor.

Fantast: July, 1942: vol. 3 no. 2

WHACKY

THE telephone honked melodiously. He picked it up and after a moment's hesitation asked 'Hello – is that me?' The answer he had been fearing came back. 'You, it is. Who are you?' He sighed: argument was useless – besides he knew he was in the wrong. 'All right,' he said wearily. 'You win.' A sudden purple twinge of toothache nearly choked him for a moment and he added hopelessly: 'Don't forget to have that stopping seen to this afternoon.' 'Ouch! as if I would,' growled the voice testily. There was a pause. 'Well, what do you want me to do now?' he asked at last. The reply, though half expected, was chilling. 'Do? It doesn't matter. You just *aren't*!'

'The amazing affair of the Elastic Sided Eggwhisk,' said the Great Detective, 'would no doubt have remained unsolved to this very day, if by great misfortune it had ever occurred. The fact that it didn't I count as one of my luckiest escapes.'

Those of us who possessed heads nodded in agreement.

He paused to drain the sump of his hookah, then continued.

'But even that fades into insignificance before the horrible tragedy that occurred in the House Where the Aspidistra Ran Amok. Fortunately I was not born at the time: otherwise I should certainly have been one of the victims.'

We shuddered in assent. Some of us had been there. Some of us were still there.

'Weren't you connected with the curious case of the Camphorated Kipper?'

He coughed deprecatingly.

39

'Intimately. I *was* the Camphorated Kipper.'

At this point two men arrived to carry me back to the taxidermist's, so I cannot tell you any more.

'Phew!' said the man in the pink silk pyjamas. 'I had a horrid dream last night!'

'Oh?' said the other disinterestedly.

'Yes – I thought that my wife had poisoned me for the insurance. It was so vivid I was mighty glad when I woke up.'

'Indeed?' said his companion politely. 'And just *where* do you think you are right now?'

CASTAWAY

'Most of the matter in the universe is at temperatures so high that no chemical compounds can exist, and the atoms themselves are stripped of all but their inner electron screens. Only on those incredibly rare bodies known as planets can the familiar elements and their combinations exist and, in all still rarer cases, give rise to the phenomenon known as life.' – *Practically any astronomy book of the early 20th Century.*

THE storm was still rising. He had long since ceased to struggle against it, although the ascending gas streams were carrying him into the bitterly cold regions ten thousand miles above his normal level. Dimly he was aware of his mistake: he should never have entered the area of disturbance, but the spot had developed so swiftly that there was now no chance of escape. The million-miles-an-hour wind had seized him as it rose from the depths and was carrying him up the great funnel it had torn in the photosphere – a tunnel already large enough to engulf a hundred worlds.

It was very cold. Around him carbon vapour was condensing in clouds of incandescent dust, swiftly torn away by the raging winds. This was something he had never met before, but the short-lived particles of solid matter left no sensation as they whipped through his body. Presently they were no more than glowing streamers far below, their furious movement foreshortened to a gentle undulation.

He was now at a truly enormous height, and his velocity showed no signs of slackening. The horizon was almost fifty thousand miles away, and the whole of the great spot lay visible beneath. Although he possessed neither eyes nor organs of sight, the radiation pattern sweeping through his body built up a picture of the awesome scene below. Like a great wound through which the Sun's life was ebbing into space, the vortex was now thousands of miles deep. From one edge a long tongue of flame was reaching out to form a half-completed bridge, defying the gales sweeping vertically past it. In a few hours, if it survived, it might span the abyss and divide the spot in twain. The fragments would drift apart, the fires of the photosphere would overwhelm them, and soon the great globe would be unblemished again.

The Sun was still receding, and gradually into his slow, dim consciousness came the understanding that he could never return. The eruption that had hurled him into space had not given him sufficient velocity to escape forever, but a second giant force was beginning to exert its power. All his life he had been subjected to the fierce bombardment of solar radiation, pouring upon him from all directions. It was doing so no longer. The Sun now lay far beneath, and the force of its radiation was driving him out into space like a mighty wind. The cloud of ions that was his body, more tenuous than air, was falling swiftly into the outer darkness.

Now the Sun was a globe of fire shrinking far behind, and the great spot no more than a black stain near the centre of its disc. Ahead lay darkness, utterly unrelieved, for his senses were far too coarse ever to detect the feeble light of the stars or the pale gleam of the circling planets. The only course of light he could ever know was dwindling from him. In a desperate effort to conserve his energy, he drew his body together into a tight, spherical cloud. Now he was almost as dense as air, but the electrostatic repulsion between his billions of constituent ions was too great for further concentration. When at last his strength weakened, they would disperse into space and no trace of his existence would remain.

He never felt the increasing gravitational pull from far ahead, and was unconscious of his changing speed. But presently the first faint intimations of the approaching magnetic field reached his consciousness and stirred it into sluggish life. He strained his senses out into the darkness, but to a creature whose home was the photosphere of the Sun the light of all other bodies was billions of times too faint even to be glimpsed, and the steadily strengthening field through which he was falling was an enigma beyond the comprehension of his rudimentary mind.

The tenuous outer fringes of the atmosphere checked his speed, and he fell slowly towards the invisible planet. Twice he felt a strange, tearing wrench as he passed through the ionosphere; then, no faster than a falling snowflake, he was drifting down through the cold, dense gas of the lower air. The descent took many hours and his strength was waning when he came to rest on a surface hard beyond anything he had ever imagined.

The waters of the Atlantic were bathed with brilliant sunlight, but to him the darkness was absolute save for the faint gleam of the infinitely distant Sun. For aeons he lay, incapable of movement, while the fires of consciousness burned lower within him and the last remnants of his energy ebbed away into the inconceivable cold.

It was long before he noticed the strange new radiation pulsing far off in the darkness – radiation of a kind he had never experienced before. Sluggishly he turned his mind towards it, considering what it might be and whence it came. It was closer than he had thought, for its movement was clearly visible and now it was climbing into the sky, approaching the Sun itself. But this was no second sun, for the strange illumination was waxing and waning, and only for a fraction of a cycle was it shining full upon him.

Nearer and nearer came that enigmatic glare; and as the throbbing rhythm of its brilliance grew fiercer he became aware of a strange, tearing resonance that seemed to shake the whole of his being. Now it was beating down upon him like a flail, tearing into his vitals and loosening · his last hold on life itself. He had lost all control over the outer regions of his compressed but still enormous body.

The end came swiftly. The intolerable radiance was directly overhead, no longer pulsing but pouring down upon him in one continuous flood. Then there was neither pain nor wonder, nor the dull longing for the great golden world he had lost forever ...

From the streamlined fairing beneath the great flying-wing, the long pencil of the radar beam was sweeping the Atlantic to the horizon's edge. Spinning in synchronism on the Plan Position Indicator, the faintly visible line of the time-base built up a picture of all that lay beneath. At the moment the screen was empty, for the coast of Ireland was more than three hundred miles away. Apart from an occasional brilliant blue spot – which was all that the greatest surface vessel became from fifty thousand feet – nothing would be visible until, in three hours' time, the eastern seaboard of America began to drift into the picture.

The navigator, checking his position continually by the North Atlantic radio lattice, seldom had any need for this part of the liner's radar. But to the passengers, the big skiatron indicator on the promenade deck was a source of constant interest, especially when the weather was bad and there was nothing to be seen below but the undulating hills and valleys of the cloud ceiling. There was still something magical, even in this age, about a radar landfall. No matter how often one had seen it before, it was fascinating to watch the pattern of the coastline forming on the screen, to pick out the harbours and the shipping and, presently, the hills and rivers and lakes of the land beneath.

To Edward Lindsey, returning from a week's leave in Europe, the Plan Position Indicator had a double interest. Fifteen years ago, as a young Coastal Command radio observer in the War of Liberation, he had spent long and tiring hours over these same waters, peering into a primitive forerunner of the great five-foot screen before him. He smiled wryly as his mind went back to those days. What would he have thought then, he wondered, if he could have seen himself as he was now, a prosperous accountant, travelling in comfort ten miles above the Atlantic at almost the velocity of sound? He thought also of the rest of S for Sugar's crew, and wondered what had happened to them in the intervening years.

At the edge of the scan, just crossing the three-hundred-mile range circle, a faint patch of light was beginning to drift into the picture. That was strange: there was no land there, for the Azores were further to the south. Besides, this seemed too ill-defined to be an island. The only thing it could possibly be was a storm-cloud heavy with rain.

Lindsey walked to the nearest window and looked out. The weather was extraordinarily fine. Far below, the waters of the Atlantic were crawling eastward towards Europe; even down to the horizon the sky was blue and cloudless.

He went back to the P.P.I. The echo was certainly a very curious one, approximately oval and as far as he could judge about ten miles long, although it was still too far away for accurate measurement. Lindsey did some rapid mental arithmetic. In twenty-five minutes it should be almost underneath them, for it was neatly bisected by the bright line that represented the aircraft's heading. Track? Course? Lord, how quickly one forgot that sort of thing! But it didn't matter – the wind could make little difference at the speed they were travelling. He would come back and

45

have a look at it then, unless the gang in the bar got hold of him again.

Twenty minutes later he was even more puzzled. The tiny blue oval of light gleaming on the dark face of the screen was now only fifty miles away. If it were indeed a cloud, it was the strangest one he had ever seen. But the scale of the picture was still too small for him to make out any details.

The main controls of the indicator were safely locked away beneath the notice which read: PASSENGERS ARE RE-QUESTED NOT TO PLACE EMPTY GLASSES ON THE SKIATRON. However, one control had been left for the use of all comers. A massive three-position switch – guaranteed unbreakable – enabled anyone to select the tube's three different ranges: three hundred, fifty, and ten miles. Normally the three-hundred-miles picture was used, but the more restricted fifty-mile scan gave much greater detail and was excellent for sightseeing overland. The ten-mile range was quite useless and no one knew why it was there.

Lindsey turned the switch to 50, and the picture seemed to explode. The mysterious echo, which had been nearing the screen's centre, now lay at its edge once more, enlarged six-fold. Lindsey waited until the afterglow of the old picture had died away; then he leaned over and carefully examined the new.

The echo almost filled the gap between the forty- and fifty-mile range circles, and now that he could see it clearly its strangeness almost took his breath away. From its centre radiated a curious network of filaments, while at its heart glowed a bright area perhaps two miles in length. It could only be fancy – yet he could have sworn that the central spot was pulsing very slowly.

Almost unable to believe his eyes, Lindsey stared into the screen. He watched in hypnotized fascination until the oval mist was less than forty miles away; then he ran to the nearest telephone and called for one of the ship's radio officers. While he was waiting, he went again to the observation port and looked out at the ocean beneath. He could see for at least a hundred miles – but there was absolutely nothing there but the blue Atlantic and the open sky.

It was a long walk from the control room to the promenade deck, and when Sub-Lieutenant Armstrong arrived, concealing his annoyance beneath a mask of polite but not obsequious service, the object was less than twenty miles away. Lindsey pointed to the skiatron.

'Look!' he said simply.

Sub-Lieutenant Armstrong looked. For a moment there was silence. Then came a curious, half-strangled ejaculation and he jumped back as if he had been stung. He leaned forward again and rubbed at the screen with his sleeve as if trying to remove something that shouldn't be there. Stopping himself in time, he grinned foolishly at Lindsey. Then he went to the observation window.

'There's nothing there. I've looked,' said Lindsey.

After the initial shock, Armstrong moved with commendable speed. He ran back to the skiatron, unlocked the controls with his master key and made a series of swift adjustments. At once the time-base began to whirl round at a greatly increased speed, giving a more continuous picture than before.

It was much clearer now. The bright nucleus *was* pulsating, and faint knots of light were moving slowly outward along the radiating filaments. As he stared, fascinated, Lindsey suddenly remembered a glimpse he had once of an amoeba under the microscope. Apparently the same thought had occurred to the Sub-Lieutenant.

'It – it looks alive!' he whispered incredulously.

'I know,' said Lindsey. 'What do you think it is?'

The other hesitated for a while. 'I remember reading

47

once that Appleton or someone had detected patches of ionization low down in the atmosphere. That's the only thing it can be.'

'But its structure! How do you explain that?'

The other shrugged his shoulders. 'I can't,' he said bluntly.

It was vertically beneath them now, disappearing into the blind area at the centre of the screen. While they were waiting for it to emerge again they had another look at the ocean below. It was uncanny; there was still absolutely nothing to be seen. But the radar could not lie. Something *must* be there —

It was fading fast when it reappeared a minute later, fading as if the full power of the radar transmitter had destroyed its cohesion. For the filaments were breaking up, and even as they watched the ten-mile-long oval began to disintegrate. There was something awe-inspiring about the sight, and for some unfathomable reason Lindsey felt a surge of pity, as though he were witnessing the death of some gigantic beast. He shook his head angrily, but he could not get the thought out of his mind.

Twenty miles away, the last traces of ionization were dispersing to the winds. Soon eye and radar screen alike saw only the unbroken waters of the Atlantic rolling endlessly eastwards as if no power could ever disturb them.

And across the screen of the great indicator, two men stared speechlessly at one another, each afraid to guess what lay in the other's mind.

HISTORY LESSON

No one could remember when the tribe had begun its long journey. The land of great rolling plains that had been its first home was now no more than a half-forgotten dream.

For many years Shann and his people had been fleeing through a country of low hills and sparkling lakes, and now the mountains lay ahead. This summer they must cross them to the southern lands. There was little time to lose. The white terror that had come down from the Poles, grinding continents to dust and freezing the very air before it, was less than a day's march behind.

Shann wondered if the glaciers could climb the mountains ahead, and within his heart he dared to kindle a little flame of hope. This might prove a barrier against which even the remorseless ice would batter in vain. In the southern lands of which the legends spoke, his people might find refuge at last.

It took weeks to discover a pass through which the tribe and the animals could travel. When midsummer came, they had camped in a lonely valley where the air was thin and the stars shone with a brilliance no one had ever seen before.

The summer was waning when Shann took his two sons and went ahead to explore the way. For three days they climbed, and for three nights slept as best they could on the freezing rocks, and on the fourth morning there was nothing ahead but a gentle rise to a cairn of grey stones built by other travellers, centuries ago.

Shann felt himself trembling, and not with cold, as they walked towards the little pyramid of stones. His sons had fallen behind. No one spoke, for too much was at stake. In a little while they would know if all their hopes had been betrayed.

To east and west, the wall of mountains curved away as if embracing the land beneath. Below lay endless miles of undulating plain, with a great river swinging across it in tremendous loops. It was a fertile land; one in which the tribe could raise crops knowing that there would be no need to flee before the harvest.

Then Shann lifted his eyes to the south, and saw the doom of all his hopes. For there at the edge of the world glimmered that deadly light he had seen so often to the north – the glint of ice below the horizon.

There was no way forward. Through all the years of flight, the glaciers from the south had been advancing to meet them. Soon they would be crushed beneath the moving walls of ice ...

Southern glaciers did not reach the mountains until a generation later. In that last summer the sons of Shann carried the sacred treasures of the tribe to the lonely cairn overlooking the plain. The ice that had once gleamed below the horizon was now almost at their feet. By spring it would be splintering against the mountain walls.

No one understood the treasures now. They were from a past too distant for the understanding of any man alive. Their origins were lost in the mists that surrounded the Golden Age, and how they had come at last into the possession of this wandering tribe was a story that now would never be told. For it was the story of a civilization that had passed beyond recall.

Once, all these pitiful relics had been treasured for some good reason, and now they had become sacred though their meaning had long been lost. The print in the old books had faded centuries ago though much of the lettering was still visible – if there had been any to read it. But many generations had passed since anyone had had a use for a set of seven-figure logarithms, an atlas of the world, and the score of Sibelius' Seventh Symphony printed, according to the flyleaf, by H. K. Chu and Sons, at the City of Pekin in the year 2371 A.D.

The old books were placed reverently in the little crypt that had been made to receive them. There followed a motley collection of fragments – gold and platinum coins, a broken telephoto lens, a watch, a coldlight lamp, a microphone, the cutter from an electric razor, some midget radio tubes, the flotsam that had been left behind when the great tide of civilization had ebbed forever.

All these treasures were carefully stowed away in their resting place. Then came three more relics, the most sacred of all because the least understood.

The first was a strangely shaped piece of metal, showing the colouration of intense heat. It was, in its way, the most pathetic of all these symbols from the past, for it told of man's greatest achievement and of the future he might have known. The mahogany stand on which it was mounted bore a silver plate with the inscription:

Auxiliary Igniter from Starboard Jet
Spaceship 'Morning Star'
Earth-Moon, A.D. 1985

Next followed another miracle of the ancient science – a sphere of transparent plastic with strangely shaped pieces of metal imbedded in it. At its centre was a tiny capsule of synthetic radio-element, surrounded by the converting screens that shifted its radiation far down the spectrum. As long as the material remained active, the sphere would be a tiny radio transmitter, broadcasting power in all directions. Only a few of these spheres had ever been made. They had been designed as perpetual beacons to mark the orbits

51

of the asteroids. But man had never reached the asteroids and the beacons had never been used.

Last of all was a flat, circular tin, wide in comparison with its depth. It was heavily sealed, and rattled when shaken. The tribal lore predicted that disaster would follow if it was ever opened, and no one knew that it held one of the great works of art of nearly a thousand years before.

The work was finished. The two men rolled the stones back into place and slowly began to descend the mountainside. Even to the last, man had given some thought to the future and had tried to preserve something for posterity.

That winter the great waves of ice began their first assault on the mountains, attacking from north and south. The foothills were overwhelmed in the first onslaught, and the glaciers ground them into dust. But the mountains stood firm, and when the summer came the ice retreated for a while.

So, winter after winter, the battle continued, and the roar of the avalanches, the grinding of rock and the explosions of splintering ice filled the air with tumult. No war of man's had been fiercer than this, and even man's battles had not quite engulfed the globe as this had done.

At last the tidal waves of ice began to subside and to creep slowly down the flanks of the mountains they had never quite subdued. The valleys and passes were still firmly in their grip. It was stalemate. The glaciers had met their match, but their defeat was too late to be of any use to man.

So the centuries passed, and presently there happened something that must occur once at least in the history of every world in the universe, no matter how remote and lonely it may be.

The ship from Venus came five thousand years too late, but its crew knew nothing of this. While still many millions of miles away, the telescopes had seen the great shroud of ice that made Earth the most brilliant object in the sky next to the sun itself.

Here and there the dazzling sheet was marred by black specks that revealed the presence of almost buried mountains. That was all. The rolling oceans, the plains and forests, the deserts and lakes – all that had been the world of man was sealed beneath the ice, perhaps forever.

The ship closed in to Earth and established an orbit less than a thousand miles away. For five days it circled the planet, while cameras recorded all that was left to see and a hundred instruments gathered information that would give the Venusian scientists many years of work.

An actual landing was not intended. There seemed little purpose in it. But on the sixth day the picture changed. A panoramic monitor, driven to the limit of its amplification, detected the dying radiation of the five-thousand-year-old beacon. Through all the centuries, it had been sending out its signals with everfailing strength as its radioactive heart steadily weakened.

The monitor locked on the beacon frequency. In the control room, a bell clamoured for attention. A little later, the Venusian ship broke free from its orbit and slanted down towards Earth, towards a range of mountains that still towered proudly above the ice, and to a cairn of grey stones that the years had scarcely touched ...

The great disc of the sun blazed fiercely in a sky no longer veiled with mist, for the clouds that had once hidden Venus had now completely gone. Whatever force had caused the change in the sun's radiation had doomed one civilization, but had given birth to another. Less than five thousand years before, the half-savage people of Venus had seen sun and stars for the first time. Just as the science of Earth had begun with astronomy, so had that of Venus, and on the warm, rich world that man had never seen progress had been incredibly rapid.

Perhaps the Venusians had been lucky. They never knew the Dark Age which had held man enchained for a thousand years. They missed the long detour into chemistry and mechanics but came at once to the more fundamental laws of radiation physics. In the time that man had taken to progress from the Pyramids to the rocket-propelled spaceship, the Venusians had passed from the discovery of agriculture to antigravity itself – the ultimate secret that man had never learned.

The warm ocean that still bore most of the young planet's life rolled its breakers languidly against the sandy shore. So new was this continent that the very sands were coarse and gritty. There had not yet been time enough for the sea to wear them smooth.

The scientists lay half in the water, their beautiful reptilian bodies gleaming in the sunlight. The greatest minds of Venus had gathered on this shore from all the islands of the planet. What they were going to hear they did not know, except that it concerned the Third World and the mysterious race that had peopled it before the coming of the ice.

The Historian was standing on the land, for the instruments he wished to use had no love of water. By his side was a large machine which attracted many curious glances from his colleagues. It was clearly concerned with optics, for a lens system projected from it towards a screen of white material a dozen yards away.

The Historian began to speak. Briefly he recapitulated what little had been discovered concerning the Third Planet and its people.

He mentioned the centuries of fruitless research that had failed to interpret a single word of the writings of Earth. The planet had been inhabited by a race of great technical ability. That, at least, was proved by the few pieces of

54

machinery that had been found in the cairn upon the mountain.

'We do not know why so advanced a civilization came to an end,' he observed. 'Almost certainly, it had sufficient knowledge to survive an Ice Age. There must have been some other factor of which we know nothing. Possibly disease or racial degeneration may have been responsible. It has been suggested that the tribal conflicts endemic to our own species in prehistoric times may have continued on the Third Planet after the coming of technology.

'Some philosophers maintain that knowledge of machinery does not necessarily imply a high degree of civilization, and it is theoretically possible to have wars in a society possessing mechanical power, flight, and even radio. Such a conception is alien to our thoughts, but we must admit its possibility. It would certainly account for the downfall of the lost race.

'It has always been assumed that we should never know anything of the physical form of the creatures who lived on Planet Three. For centuries our artists have been depicting scenes from the history of the dead world, peopling it with all manner of fantastic beings. Most of these creations have resembled us more or less closely, though it has often been pointed out that because *we* are reptiles it does not follow that all intelligent life must necessarily be reptilian.

'We now know the answer to one of the most baffling problems of history. At last, after hundreds of years of research, we have discovered the exact form and nature of the ruling life on the Third Planet.'

There was a murmur of astonishment from the assembled scientists. Some were so taken aback that they disappeared for a while into the comfort of the ocean, as all Venusians were apt to do in moments of stress. The Historian waited until his colleagues re-emerged into the element they so disliked. He himself was quite comfortable, thanks to the tiny sprays that were continually playing over his body. With their help he could live on land for many hours before having to return to the ocean.

The excitement slowly subsided and the lecturer continued:

'One of the most puzzling of the objects found on Planet Three was a flat metal container holding a great length of transparent plastic material, perforated at the edges and wound tightly into a spool. This transparent tape at first seemed quite featureless, but an examination with the new subelectronic microscope has shown that this is not the case. Along the surface material, invisible to our eyes but perfectly clear under the correct radiation, are literally thousands of tiny pictures. It is believed they were imprinted on the material by some chemical means, and have faded with the passage of time.

'These pictures apparently form a record of life as it was on the Third Planet at the height of its civilization. They are not independent. Consecutive pictures are almost identical, differing only in the detail of movement. The purpose of such a record is obvious. It is only necessary to project the scenes in rapid succession to give an illusion of continuous movement. We have made a machine to do this, and I have here an exact reproduction of the picture sequence.

'The scenes you are now going to witness take us back many thousands of years, to the great days of our sister planet. They show a complex civilization, many of whose activities we can only dimly understand. Life seems to have been very violent and energetic, and much that you will see is quite baffling.

'It is clear that the Third Planet was inhabited by a number of different species, none of them reptilian. That is a blow to our pride, but the conclusion is inescapable. The dominant type of life appears to have been a two-armed biped. It walked upright and covered its body with some flexible material, possibly for protection against the cold, since even before the Ice Age the planet was at a much lower temperature than our own world. But I will not try your patience any further. You will now see the record of which I have been speaking.'

A brilliant light flashed from the projector. There was a gentle whirring, and on the screen appeared hundreds of strange beings moving rather jerkily to and fro. The picture expanded to embrace one of the creatures, and the scientists could see that the Historian's description had been correct.

The creature possessed two eyes, set rather close together, but the other facial adornments were a little obscure. There was a large orifice in the lower portion of the head that was continually opening and closing. Possibly it had something to do with the creature's breathing.

The scientists watched spellbound as the strange being became involved in a series of fantastic adventures. There was an incredibly violent conflict with another, slightly different creature. It seemed certain that they must both be killed, but when it was all over neither seemed any the worse.

Then came a furious drive over miles of country in a four-wheeled mechanical devise which was capable of extraordinary feats of locomotion. The ride ended in a city packed with other vehicles moving in all directions at breathtaking speeds. No one was surprised to see two of the machines meet head-on with devastating results.

After that, events became even more complicated. It was now quite obvious that it would take many years of research to analyse and understand all that was happening. It was also clear that the record was a work of art, somewhat stylized, rather than an exact reproduction of life as it actually had been on the Third Planet.

Most of the scientists felt themselves completely dazed when the sequence of pictures came to an end. There was a final flurry of motion, in which the creature that had been the centre of interest became involved in some tremendous but incomprehensible catastrophe. The picture contracted to a circle, centred on the creature's head.

The last scene of all was an expanded view of its face, obviously expressing some powerful emotion. But whether it was rage, grief, defiance, resignation or some other feeling could not be guessed. The picture vanished. For a moment some lettering appeared on the screen, then it was all over.

For several minutes there was complete silence, save for the lapping of the waves upon the sand. The scientists were too stunned to speak. The fleeting glimpse of Earth's civilization had had a shattering effect on their minds. Then little groups began to start talking together, first in whispers and then more and more loudly as the implications of what they had seen became clearer. Presently the Historian called for attention and addressed the meeting again.

'We are now planning,' he said, 'a vast programme of research to extract all available knowledge from this record. Thousands of copies are being made for distribution to all workers. You will appreciate the problem involved. The psychologists in particular have an immense task confronting them.

'But I do not doubt that we shall succeed. In another generation, who can say what we may not have learned of this wonderful race? Before we leave, let us look again at our remote cousins, whose wisdom may have surpassed our own but of whom so little has survived.'

Once more the final picture flashed on the screen, motionless this time, for the projector had been stopped. With something like awe, the scientists gazed at the still figure from the past, while in turn the little biped stared

58

back at them with its characteristic expression of arrogant bad temper.

For the rest of time it would symbolize the human race. The psychologists of Venus would analyze its actions and watch its every movement until they could reconstruct its mind. Thousands of books would be written about it. Intricate philosophies would be contrived to account for its behaviour.

But all this labour, all this research, would be utterly in vain. Perhaps the proud and lonely figure on the screen was smiling sardonically at the scientists who were starting on their age-long fruitless quest.

Its secret would be safe as long as the universe endured, for no one now would ever read the lost language of Earth. Millions of times in the ages to come those last few words would flash across the screen, and none could ever guess their meaning:

A Walt Disney Production.

HIDE AND SEEK

WE were walking back through the woods when Kingman saw the grey squirrel. Our bag was a small but varied one – three grouse, four rabbits (one, I am sorry to say, an infant in arms) and a couple of pigeons. And contrary to certain dark forecasts, both the dogs were still alive.

The squirrel saw us at the same moment. It knew that it was marked for immediate execution as a result of the damage it had done to the trees on the estate, and perhaps it had lost close relatives to Kingman's gun. In three leaps it had reached the base of the nearest tree, and vanished behind it in a flicker of grey. We saw its face once more, appearing for a moment round the edge of its shield a dozen feet from the ground; but though we waited, with guns levelled hopefully at various branches, we never saw it again.

Kingman was very thoughtful as we walked back across the lawn to the magnificent old house. He said nothing as we handed our victims to the cook – who received them without much enthusiasm – and only emerged from his reverie when we were sitting in the smoking room and he remembered his duties as a host.

'That tree-rat,' he said suddenly (he always called them 'tree rats', on the grounds that people were too sentimental to shoot the dear little squirrels) 'it reminded me of a very peculiar experience that happened shortly before I retired. Very shortly indeed, in fact.'

'I thought it would,' said Carson dryly. I gave him a glare: he'd been in the Navy and had heard Kingman's stories before, but they were still new to me.

'Of course,' Kingman remarked, slightly nettled, 'if you'd rather I didn't . . .'

'Do go on,' I said hastily. 'You've made me curious. What connexion there can possibly be between a grey squirrel and the Second Jovian War I can't imagine.'

Kingman seemed mollified.

'I think I'd better change some names,' he said thoughtfully, 'but I won't alter the places. The story begins about a million kilometres sunward of Mars . . .'

K.15 was a military intelligence operative. It gave him considerable pain when unimaginative people called him a spy, but at the moment he had much more substantial grounds for complaint. For some days now a fast enemy cruiser had been coming up astern and though it was flattering to have the undivided attention of such a fine ship and so many highly trained men, it was an honour that K.15 would willingly have foregone.

What made the situation doubly annoying was the fact that his friends would be meeting him off Mars in about twelve hours, aboard a ship capable of dealing with a mere cruiser – from which you will gather that K.15 was a person of some importance. Unfortunately, the most optimistic calculation showed that the pursuers would be within accurate gun range in six hours. In some six hours five minutes, therefore, K.15 was likely to occupy an extensive and still expanding volume of space.

There might just be time for him to land on Mars, but that would be one of the worst things he could do. It would certainly annoy the aggressively neutral Martians, and the political complications would be frightful. Moreover, if his friends *had* to come down to the planet to rescue him, it would cost them more than ten kilometres a second in fuel – most of their operational reserve.

He had only one advantage, and that a very dubious one.

The Commander of the cruiser might guess that he was heading for a rendezvous, but he would not know how close it was or how large was the ship that was coming to meet him. If he could keep alive for only twelve hours, he would be safe. The 'if' was a somewhat considerable one.

K.15 looked moodily at his charts, wondering if it was worth while to burn the rest of his fuel in a final dash. But a dash to where? He would be completely helpless then, and the pursuing ship might still have enough in her tanks to catch him as he flashed outward into the empty darkness, beyond all hope of rescue – passing his friends as they came sunward at a relative speed so great that they could do nothing to save him.

With some people, the shorter the expectation of life, the more sluggish are the mental processes. They seem hypnotized by the approach of death, so resigned to their fate that they do nothing to avoid it. K.15, on the other hand, found that his mind worked better in such a desperate emergency. It began to work now as it had seldom done before.

Commander Smith – the name will do as well as any other – of the cruiser *Doradus* was not unduly surprised when K.15 began to decelerate. He had half expected the spy to land on Mars, on the principle that internment was better than annihilation, but when the plotting room brought the news that the little scout ship was heading for Phobos, he felt completely baffled. The inner moon was nothing but a jumble of rocks some twenty kilometres across, and not even the economical Martians had ever found any use for it. K.15 must be pretty desperate if he thought it was going to be of any greater value to him.

The tiny scout had almost come to rest when the radar operator lost it against the mass of Phobos. During the braking manoeuvre, K.15 had squandered most of his lead and the *Doradus* was now only minutes away – though she was now beginning to decelerate lest she overrun him. The cruiser was scarcely three thousand kilometres from Phobos when she came to a complete halt: of K.15's ship, there was still no sign. It should be easily visible in the telescopes, but it was probably on the far side of the little moon.

It reappeared only a few minutes later, travelling under full thrust on a course directly away from the sun. It was accelerating at almost five gravities – and it had broken its radio silence. An automatic recorder was broadcasting over and over again this interesting message:

'I have landed on Phobos and am being attacked by a Z-class cruiser. Think I can hold out until you come, but hurry.'

The message wasn't even in code, and it left Commander Smith a sorely puzzled man. The assumption that K.15 was still aboard the ship and that the whole thing was a ruse was just a little too naïve. But it might be a double-bluff: the message had obviously been left in plain language so that he would receive it and be duly confused. He could afford neither the time nor the fuel to chase the scout if K.15 really had landed. It was clear that reinforcements were on the way, and the sooner he left the vicinity the better. The phrase 'Think I can hold out until you come' might be a piece of sheer impertinence, or it might mean that help was very near indeed.

Then K.15's ship stopped blasting. It had obviously exhausted its fuel, and was doing a little better than six kilometres a second away from the sun. K.15 *must* have landed, for his ship was now speeding helplessly out of the solar system. Commander Smith didn't like the message it was broadcasting, and guessed that it was running into the track of an approaching warship at some indefinite distance, but there was nothing to be done about that. The *Doradus* began to move towards Phobos, anxious to waste no time.

On the face of it, Commander Smith seemed the master of the situation. His ship was armed with a dozen heavy guided missiles and two turrets of electro-magnetic guns. Against him was one man in a spacesuit, trapped on a moon only twenty kilometres across. It was not until the Commander had his first good look at Phobos, from a distance of less than a hundred kilometres, that he began to realize that, after all, K.15 might have a few cards up his sleeve.

To say that Phobos has a diameter of twenty kilometres, as the astronomy books invariably do, is highly misleading. The word 'diameter' implies a degree of symmetry which Phobos most certainly lacks. Like those other lumps of cosmic slag, the asteroids, it is a shapeless mass of rock floating in space with, of course, no hint of an atmosphere and not much more gravity. It turns on its axis once every seven hours thirty-nine minutes, thus keeping the same face always to Mars – which is so close that appreciably less than half the planet is visible, the poles being below the curve of the horizon. Beyond this, there is very little more to be said about Phobos.

K.15 had not time to enjoy the beauty of the crescent world filling the sky above him. He had thrown all the equipment he could carry out of the airlock, set the controls, and jumped. As the little ship went flaming out towards the stars he watched it go with feelings he did not care to analyse. He had burned his boats with a vengeance, and he could only hope that the oncoming battleship would intercept the radio message as the empty vessel went racing by into nothingness. There was also a faint possibility that the enemy cruiser might go in pursuit, but that was rather too much to hope for.

He turned to examine his new home. The only light was the ochre radiance of Mars, since the sun was below the horizon, but it was quite sufficient for his purpose and he could see very well. He stood in the centre of an irregular plain about two kilometres across, surrounded by low hills over which he could leap rather easily if he wished. There was a story he remembered reading long ago about a man who had accidentally jumped off Phobos: that wasn't quite possible – though it was on Deimos – as the escape velocity was still about ten metres a second. But unless he was careful, he might easily find himself at such a height that it would take hours to fall back to the surface – and that would be fatal. For K.15's plan was a simple one: he must remain as close to the surface of Phobos as possible – *and diametrically opposite the cruiser*. The *Doradus* was armed with the latest in ultra-scientific weapons: moreover, the twenty kilometres which separated her from her prey represented less than a second's flight at maximum speed. But Commander Smith knew better, and was already feeling rather unhappy. He realized, only too well, that of all the machines of transport man had invented, a cruiser of space is far and away the least manoeuvrable. It was a simple fact that K.15 could make half a dozen circuits of his little world while her commander was persuading the *Doradus* to make one.

There is no need to go into technical details, but those who are still unconvinced might like to consider these elementary facts. A rocket-driven spaceship can, obviously, only accelerate along its major axis – that is, 'forward'. Any deviation from a straight course demands a physical turning of the ship, so that the motors can blast in another direction. Everyone knows that this is done by internal gyros or tangential steering jets, but very few people know just how long this simple manoeuvre takes. The average cruiser, fully fuelled, has a mass of two or three thousand tons, which does not make for rapid footwork. But things are even worse than this, for it isn't the mass, but the moment of inertia that matters here – and since a cruiser is a long, thin object, its moment of inertia is slightly colossal. The sad fact remains (though it is seldom mentioned by astronautical engineers) that it takes a good ten minutes to rotate a spaceship through 180 degrees, with gyros of any reasonable size. Control jets aren't much quicker, and in any case their use is restricted because the rotation they produce is permanent and they are liable to leave the ship spinning like a slow motion pinwheel, to the annoyance of all inside.

In the ordinary way, these disadvantages are not very grave. One has millions of kilometres and hundreds of hours in which to deal with such minor matters as a change in the ship's orientation. It is definitely against the rules to move in ten-kilometre radius circles, and the Commander of the *Doradus* felt distinctly aggrieved. K.15 wasn't playing fair.

At the same moment that resourceful individual was taking stock of the situation, which might very well have been worse. He had reached the hills in three jumps and felt less naked than he had out in the open plain. The food and equipment he had taken from the ship he had hidden where he hoped he could find it again, but as his suit could keep him alive for over a day that was the least of his worries. The small packet that was the cause of all the trouble was still with him, in one of those numerous hiding places a well-designed space-suit affords.

There was an exhilarating loneliness about his mountain eyrie, even though he was not quite as lonely as he would have wished. Forever fixed in his sky, Mars was waning almost visibly as Phobos swept above the night side of the planet. He could just make out the lights of some of the Martian cities, gleaming pin-points marking the junctions of the invisible canals. All else was stars and silence and a line of jagged peaks so close it seemed he could almost touch them. Of the *Doradus* there was still no sign. She was presumably carrying out a careful telescopic examination of the sunlit side of Phobos.

Mars was a very useful clock: when it was half full the sun would rise and, very probably, so would the *Doradus*. But she might approach from some quite unexpected quarter: she might even – and this was the one real danger – she might even have landed a search party.

This was the first possibility that had occurred to Commander Smith when he saw just what he was up against. Then he realized that the surface area of Phobos was over a thousand square kilometres and that he could not spare more than ten men from his crew to make a search of that jumbled wilderness. Also, K.15 would certainly be armed.

Considering the weapons which the *Doradus* carried, this last objection might seem singularly pointless. It was very far from being so. In the ordinary course of business, side-arms and other portable weapons are as much use to a space-cruiser as are cutlasses and crossbows. The *Doradus* happened, quite by chance – and against regulations at that – to carry one automatic pistol and a hundred rounds of ammunition. Any search party would therefore consist of a group of unarmed men looking for a well-concealed and very desperate individual who could pick them off at his leisure. K.15 was breaking the rules again.

The terminator of Mars was now a perfectly straight line, and at almost the same moment the sun came up, not so much like thunder as like a salvo of atomic bombs. K.15 adjusted the filters of his visor and decided to move. It was safer to stay out of the sunlight, not only because here he was less likely to be detected in the shadow but also because his eyes would be much more sensitive there. He had only a pair of binoculars to help him, whereas the *Doradus* would carry an electronic telescope of twenty centimetres aperture at least.

It would be best, K.15 decided, to locate the cruiser if

he could. It might be a rash thing to do, but he would feel much happier when he knew exactly where she was and could watch her movements. He could then keep just below the horizon, and the glare of the rockets would give him ample warning of any impending move. Cautiously launching himself along an almost horizontal trajectory, he began the circumnavigation of his world.

The narrowing crescent of Mars sank below the horizon until only one vast horn reared itself enigmatically against the stars. K.15 began to feel worried: there was still no sign of the *Doradus*. But this was hardly surprising, for she was painted black as night and might be a good hundred kilometres away in space. He stopped, wondering if he had done the right thing after all. Then he noticed that something quite large was eclipsing the stars almost vertically overhead, and was moving swiftly even as he watched. His heart stopped for a moment: then he was himself again, analysing the situation and trying to discover how he had made so disastrous a mistake.

It was some time before he realized that the black shadow slipping across the sky was not the cruiser at all, but something almost equally deadly. It was far smaller, and far nearer, than he had at first thought. The *Doradus* had sent her television-homing guided missiles to look for him.

This was the second danger he had feared, and there was nothing he could do about it except to remain as inconspicuous as possible. The *Doradus* now had many eyes searching for him, but these auxiliaries had very severe limitations. They had been built to look for sunlit spaceships against a background of stars, not to search for a man hiding in a dark jungle of rock. The definition of their television systems was low, and they could only see in the forward direction.

There were rather more men on the chessboard now, and

the game was a little deadlier, but his was still the advantage.

The torpedo vanished into the night sky. As it was travelling on a nearly straight course in this low gravitational field, it would soon be leaving Phobos behind, and K.15 waited for what he knew must happen. A few minutes later, he saw a brief stabbing of rocket exhausts and guessed the projectile was swinging slowly back on its course. At almost the same moment he saw another flare far away in the opposite quarter of the sky, and wondered just how many of these infernal machines were in action. From what he knew of Z-class cruisers – which was a good deal more than he should – there were four missile-control channels, and they were probably all in use.

He was suddenly struck by an idea so brilliant that he was quite sure it couldn't possibly work. The radio on his suit was a tunable one, covering an unusually wide band, and somewhere not far away the *Doradus* was pumping out power on everything from a thousand megacycles upward. He switched on the receiver and began to explore.

It came in quickly – the raucous whine of a pulse transmitter not far away. He was probably only picking up a subharmonic, but that was quite good enough. It D/F'ed sharply, and for the first time K.15 allowed himself to make long-range plans for the future. The *Doradus* had betrayed herself: as long as she operated her missiles, he would know exactly where she was.

He moved cautiously forward towards the transmitter. To his surprise the signal faded, then increased sharply again. This puzzled him until he realized that he must be moving through a diffraction zone. Its width might have told him something useful if he had been a good enough physicist, but he couldn't imagine what.

The *Doradus* was hanging about five kilometres above the surface, in full sunlight. Her 'non-reflecting' paint was overdue for renewal, and K.15 could see her clearly. As he was still in darkness, and the shadow line was moving away from him, he decided that he was as safe here as anywhere. He settled down comfortably so that he could just see the cruiser and waited, feeling fairly certain that none of the guided projectiles would come so near the ship. By now, he calculated, the Commander of the *Doradus* must be getting pretty mad. He was perfectly correct.

After an hour, the cruiser began to heave herself round with all the grace of a bogged hippopotamus. K.15 guessed what was happening. Commander Smith was going to have a look at the antipodes, and was preparing for the perilous fifty-kilometre journey. He watched very carefully to see the orientation the ship was adopting, and when she came to rest again was relieved to see that she was almost broadside on to him. Then, with a series of jerks that could not have been very enjoyable aboard, the cruiser began to move down to the horizon. K.15 followed her at a comfortable walking pace – if one could use the phrase – reflecting that this was a feat very few people had ever performed. He was particularly careful not to overtake her on one of his kilometre-long glides, and kept a close watch for any missiles that might be coming up astern.

It took the *Doradus* nearly an hour to cover the fifty kilometres. This, as K.15 amused himself by calculating, represented considerably less than a thousandth of her normal speed. Once she found herself going off into space at a tangent, and rather than waste time turning end over end again fired off a salvo of shells to reduce speed. But she made it at last, and K.15 settled down for another vigil, wedged between two rocks where he could just see the cruiser and he was quite sure she couldn't see him. It occurred to him that by this time Commander Smith might have grave doubts as to whether he really was on Phobos at all, and he felt like firing off a signal flare to reassure him. However, he resisted the temptation.

There would be little point in describing the events of the next ten hours, since they differed in no important detail from those that had gone before. The *Doradus* made three other moves, and K.15 stalked her with the care of a big-game hunter following the spoor of some elephantine beast. Once, when she would have led him out into full sunlight, he let her fall below the horizon until he could only just pick up her signals. But most of the time he kept her just visible, usually low down behind some convenient hill.

Once a torpedo exploded some kilometres away, and K.15 guessed that some exasperated operator had seen a shadow he didn't like – or else that a technician had forgotten to switch off a proximity fuse. Otherwise nothing happened to enliven the proceedings: in fact, the whole affair was becoming rather boring. He almost welcomed the sight of an occasional guided missile drifting inquisitively overhead, for he did not believe that they could see him if he remained motionless and in reasonable cover. If he could have stayed on the part of Phobos exactly opposite the cruiser he would have been safe even from these, he realized, since the ship would have no control there in the moon's radio-shadow. But he could think of no reliable way in which he could be sure of staying in the safety zone if the cruiser moved again.

The end came very abruptly. There was a sudden blast of steering jets, and the cruiser's main drive burst forth in all its power and splendour. In seconds the *Doradus* was shrinking sunward, free at last, thankful to leave, even in defeat, this miserable lump of rock that had so annoyingly balked her of her legitimate prey. K.15 knew what had happened, and a great sense of peace and relaxation swept over him. In the radar room of the cruiser, someone had seen an echo of disconcerting amplitude approaching with altogether excessive speed. K.15 now had only to switch on his suit beacon and to wait. He could even afford the luxury of a cigarette.

'Quite an interesting story,' I said, 'and I see now how it ties up with that squirrel. But it does raise one or two queries in my mind.'

'Indeed?' said Rupert Kingman politely.

I always like to get to the bottom of things, and I knew that my host had played a part in the Jovian War about which he very seldom spoke. I decided to risk a long shot in the dark.

'May I ask how you happen to know so much about this unorthodox military engagement? It isn't possible, is it, that *you* were K.15?'

There was an odd sort of strangling noise from Carson. Then Kingman said, quite calmly: 'No, I wasn't.'

He got to his feet and went off towards the gun room.

'If you'll excuse me a moment, I'm going to have another shot at that tree-rat. Maybe I'll get him this time.' Then he was gone.

Carson looked at me as if to say: 'This is another house you'll never be invited to again.' When our host was out of earshot he remarked in a coldly cynical voice:

'You've done it. What did you have to say that for?'

'Well, it seemed a safe guess. How else could he have known all that?'

'As a matter of fact, I believe he met K.15 after the War: they must have had an interesting conversation together. But I thought you knew that Rupert was retired from the service with only the rank of lieutenant commander. The Court of Inquiry could never see his point of view. After all, it just wasn't reasonable that the commander of the fastest ship in the Fleet couldn't catch a man in a space-suit.'

73

SECOND DAWN

'HERE they come,' said Eris, rising to his forefeet and turning to look down the long valley. For a moment the pain and bitterness had left his thoughts, so that even Jeryl, whose mind was more closely tuned to his than to any other, could scarcely detect it. There was even an undertone of softness that recalled poignantly the Eris she had known in the days before the War – the old Eris who now seemed almost as remote and as lost as if he were lying with all the others out there on the plain.

A dark tide was flowing up the valley, advancing with a curious, hesitant motion, making odd pauses and little bounds forward. It was flanked with gold – the thin line of the Atheleni guards, so terrifyingly few compared with the black mass of the prisoners. But they were enough: indeed, they were only needed to guide that aimless river on its faltering way. Yet at the sight of so many thousands of the enemy, Jeryl found herself trembling and instinctively moved towards her mate, silver pelt resting against gold. Eris gave no sign that he had understood or even noticed the action.

The fear vanished as Jeryl saw how slowly the dark flood was moving forwards. She had been told what to expect, but the reality was even worse than she had imagined. As the prisoners came nearer, all the hate and bitterness ebbed from her mind, to be replaced by a sick compassion. No one of her race need ever more fear the aimless, idiot horde that was being shepherded through the pass into the valley it would never leave again.

The guards were doing little more than urge the prisoners

on with meaningless but encouraging cries, like nurses calling to infants too young to sense their thoughts. Strain as she might, Jeryl could detect no vestige of reason in any of these thousands of minds passing so near at hand. That brought home to her, more vividly than could anything else, the magnitude of the victory – and of the defeat. Her mind was sensitive enough to detect the first faint thoughts of children, hovering on the verge of consciousness. The defeated enemy had become not even children, but babies with the bodies of adults.

The tide was passing within a few feet of them now. For the first time, Jeryl realized how much larger than her own people the Mithraneans were, and how beautifully the light of the twin suns gleamed on the dark satin of their bodies. Once a magnificent specimen, towering a full head above Eris, broke loose from the main body and came blundering towards them, halting a few paces away. Then it crouched down like a lost and frightened child, the splendid head moving uncertainly from side to side as if seeking it knew not what. For a moment the great, empty eyes fell full upon Jeryl's face. She was as beautiful, she knew, to the Mithraneans as to her own race – but there was no flicker of emotion on the blank features, and no pause in the aimless movement of the questing head. Then an exasperated guard drove the prisoner back to his fellows.

'Come away,' Jeryl pleaded. 'I don't want to see any more. Why did you ever bring me here?' The last thought was heavy with reproach.

Eris began to move away over the grassy slopes in great bounds that she could not hope to match, but as he went his mind threw its message back to hers. His thoughts were still gentle, though the pain beneath them was too deep to be concealed.

'I wanted everyone – even you – to see what we had to do to win the War. Then, perhaps, we will have no more

76

in our lifetimes.'

He was waiting for her on the brow of the hill, undistressed by the mad violence of his climb. The stream of prisoners was now too far below for them to see the details of its painful progress. Jeryl crouched down beside Eris and began to browse on the sparse vegetation that had been exiled from the fertile valley. She was slowly beginning to recover from the shock.

'But what will happen to them?' she asked presently, still haunted by the memory of that splendid, mindless giant going into a captivity it could never understand.

'They can be taught how to eat,' said Eris. 'There is food in the valley for half a year, and then we'll move them on. It will be a heavy strain on our own resources, but we're under a moral obligation – and we've put it in the peace treaty.'

'They can never be cured?'

'No. Their minds have been totally destroyed. They'll be like this until they die.'

There was a long silence. Jeryl let her gaze wander across the hills, falling in gentle undulations to the edge of the ocean. She could just make out, beyond a gap in the hills, the distant line of blue that marked the sea – the mysterious, impassable sea. Its blue would soon be deepening into darkness, for the fierce white sun was setting and presently there would only be the red disc – hundreds of times larger but giving far less light – of its pale companion.

'I suppose we had to do it,' Jeryl said at last. She was thinking almost to herself, but she let enough of her thoughts escape for Eris to overhear.

'You've seen them,' he answered briefly. 'They were bigger and stronger than we. Though we outnumbered them, it was stalemate: in the end, I think they would have won. By doing what we did, we saved thousands from death – or mutilation.'

The bitterness came back into his thoughts, and Jeryl

dared not look at him. He had screened the depths of his mind, but she knew that he was thinking of the shattered ivory stump upon his forehead. The War had been fought, except at the very end, with two weapons only – the razor-sharp hooves of the little, almost useless forepaws, and the unicornlike horns. With one of these Eris could never fight again, and from the loss stemmed much of the embittered harshness that sometimes made him hurt even those who loved him.

Eris was waiting for someone, though who it was Jeryl could not guess. She knew better than to interrupt his thoughts while he was in his present mood, and so remained silently beside him, her shadow merging with his as it stretched far along the hill-top.

Jeryl and Eris came of a race which, in Nature's lottery, had been luckier than most – and yet had missed one of the greatest prizes of all. They had powerful bodies and powerful minds, and they lived in a world which was both temperate and fertile. By human standards, they would have seemed strange but by no means repulsive. Their sleek, fur-covered bodies tapered to a single giant rear limb that could send them leaping over the ground in thirty-foot bounds. The two forelimbs were much smaller, and served merely for support and steadying. They ended in pointed hooves that could be deadly in combat, but had no other useful purpose.

Both the Atheleni and their cousins, the Mithraneans, possessed mental powers that had enabled them to develop a very advanced mathematics and philosophy: but over the physical world they had no control at all. Houses, tools, clothes – indeed, artifacts of any kind – were utterly unknown to them. To races which possessed hands, tentacles or other means of manipulation, their culture would have seemed incredibly limited: yet such is the adaptability of the mind, and the power of the commonplace, that they seldom realized their handicaps and could imagine no other way of life. It was natural to wander in great herds over the fertile plains, pausing where food was plentiful and moving on again when it was exhausted. This nomadic life had given them enough leisure for philosophy and even for certain arts. Their telepathic powers had not yet robbed them of their voices and they had developed a complex vocal music and an even more complex choreography. But they took the greatest pride of all in the range of their thoughts: for thousands of generations they had sent their minds roving through the misty infinities of metaphysics. Of *physics*, and indeed of all the sciences of matter, they knew nothing – not even that they existed.

'Someone's coming,' said Jeryl suddenly. 'Who is it?'

Eris did not bother to look, but there was a sense of strain in his reply.

'It's Aretenon. I agreed to meet him here.'

'I'm so glad. You were such good friends once – it upset me when you quarrelled.'

Eris pawed fretfully at the turf, as he did when he was embarrassed or annoyed.

'I lost my temper with him when he left me during the fifth battle of the Plain. Of course I didn't know then why he had to go.'

Jeryl's eyes widened in sudden amazement and understanding.

'You mean – he had something to do with the Madness, and the way the War ended?'

'Yes. There were very few people who knew more about the mind than he did. I don't know what part he played, but it must have been an important one. I don't suppose he'll ever be able to tell us much about it.'

Still a considerable distance below them, Aretenon was zigzagging up the hillside in great leaps. A little later he had reached them and instinctively bent his head to touch horns with Eris in the universal gesture of greeting. Then he stopped, horribly embarrassed, and there was an awkward pause until Jeryl came to the rescue with some conventional remarks.

When Eris spoke, Jeryl was relieved to sense his obvious pleasure at meeting his friend once again, for the first time since their angry parting at the height of the War. It had been longer still since her last meeting with Aretenon, and she was surprised to see how much he had changed. He was considerably younger than Eris – but no one would have guessed it now. Some of his once-golden pelt was turning black with age, and with a flash of his old humour Eris remarked that soon no one would be able to tell him from a Mithranean.

Aretenon smiled.

'That would have been useful in the last few weeks. I've just come through their country, helping to round up the Wanderers. We weren't very popular, as you might expect. If they'd known who I was, I don't suppose I'd have got back alive – armistice or no armistice.'

'You weren't actually in charge of the Madness, were you?' asked Jeryl, unable to control her curiosity.

She had a momentary impression of thick, defensive mists forming around Aretenon's mind, shielding all his thoughts from the outer world. Then the reply came, curiously muffled, and with a sense of distance that was very rare in telepathic-contact.

'No: I wasn't in supreme charge. But there were only two others between myself and – the top.'

'Of course,' said Eris, rather petulantly, 'I'm only an ordinary soldier and don't understand these things. But I'd like to know just how you did it. Naturally,' he added, 'neither Jeryl nor myself would talk to anyone else.'

Again that veil seemed to descend over Aretenon's thoughts. Then it lifted, ever so slightly.

'There's very little I'm allowed to tell. As you know, Eris, I was always interested in the mind and its workings. Do you remember the games we used to play, when I tried to uncover your thoughts, and you did your best to stop me? And how I sometimes made you carry out acts against your will?'

'I still think,' said Eris, 'that you couldn't have done that to a stranger, and that I was really unconsciously co-operating.'

'That was true then – but it isn't any longer. The proof lies down there in the valley.' He gestured towards the last stragglers who were being rounded up by the guards. The dark tide had almost passed, and soon the entrance to the valley would be closed.

'When I grew older,' continued Aretenon, 'I spent more and more of my time probing into the ways of the mind, and trying to discover why some of us can share our thoughts so easily, while others can never do so but must remain always isolated and alone, forced to communicate by sounds or gestures. And I became fascinated by those rare minds that are completely deranged, so that those who possess them seem less than children.

'I had to abandon these studies when the War began. Then, as you know, they called for me one day during the fifth battle. Even now, I'm not quite sure who was responsible for that. I was taken to a place a long way from here, where I found a little group of thinkers many of whom I already knew.

'The plan was simple – and tremendous. From the dawn of our race we've known that two or three minds, linked together, could be used to control another mind, *if it was willing,* in the way that I used to control you. We've employed this power for healing since ancient times. Now we planned to use it for destruction.

'There were two main difficulties. One was bound up

with that curious limitation of our normal telepathic powers – the fact that, except in rare cases, we can only have contact over a distance *with someone we already know*, and can communicate with strangers only when we are actually in their presence.

'The second, and greater problem, was that the massed power of many minds would be needed, and never before had it been possible to link together more than two or three. How we succeeded is our main secret: like all things, it seems easy now it has been done. And once we had started, it was simpler than we had expected. Two minds are more than twice as powerful as one, and three are much more than thrice as powerful as a single will. The exact mathematical relationship is an interesting one. You know how very rapidly the number of ways a group of objects may be arranged increases with the size of the group? Well, a similar relationship holds in this case.

'So in the end we had our Composite Mind. At first it was unstable, and we could hold it together only for a few seconds. It's still a tremendous strain on our mental resources, and even now we can only do it for – well, for long enough.

'All these experiments, of course, were carried out in great secrecy. If we could do this, so could the Mithraneans, for their minds are as good as ours. We had a number of their prisoners, and we used them as subjects.'

For a moment the veil that hid Aretenon's inner thoughts seemed to tremble and dissolve: then he regained control.

'That was the worst part. It was bad enough to send madness into a far land, but it was infinitely worse when you could watch with your own eyes the effects of what you did.

'When we had perfected our technique, we made the first long-distance test. Our victim was someone so well known to one of our prisoners – whose mind we had taken over – that we could identify him completely and thus the

82

distance between us was no objection. The experiment worked, but of course no one suspected that we were responsible.

'We did not operate again until we were certain that our attack would be so overwhelming that it would end the War. From the minds of our prisoners we had identified about a score of Mithraneans – their friends and kindred – in such detail that we could pick them out and destroy them. As each mind fell beneath our attack, it gave up to us the knowledge of others, and so our power increased. We could have done far more damage than we did, for we took only the males.'

'Was that,' said Jeryl bitterly, 'so very merciful?'

'Perhaps not: but it should be remembered to our credit. We stopped as soon as the enemy sued for peace, and as we alone knew what had happened, we went into their country to undo what damage we could. It was little enough.'

There was a long silence. The valley was deserted now, and the white sun had set. A cold wind was blowing over the hills, passing, where none could follow it, out across the empty and untravelled sea. Then Eris spoke, his thoughts almost whispering in Aretenon's mind.

'You did not come to tell me this, did you? There is something more.' It was a statement rather than a query.

'Yes,' replied Aretenon. 'I have a message for you – one that will surprise you a good deal. It's from Therodimus.'

'Therodimus! I thought —'

'You thought he was dead, or worse still, a traitor. He's neither, although he's lived in enemy territory for the last twenty years. The Mithraneans treated him as we did, and gave him everything he needed. They recognized his mind for what it was, and even during the War no one touched him. Now he wants to see you again.'

Whatever emotions Eris was feeling at this news of his old teacher, he gave no sign of them. Perhaps he was re-

83

calling his youth, remembering now that Therodimus had played a greater part in the shaping of his mind than any other single influence. But his thoughts were barred to Aretenon and even to Jeryl.

'What's he been doing all this time?' Eris asked at length. 'And why does he want to see me now?'

'It's a long and complicated story,' said Aretenon, 'but Therodimus has made a discovery quite as remarkable as ours, and one that may have even greater consequences.'

'Discovery? What sort of discovery?'

Aretenon paused, looking thoughtfully along the valley. The guards were returning, leaving behind only a few who would be needed to deal with any wandering prisoners.

'You know as much of our history as I do, Eris,' he began. 'It took, we believe, something like a million generations for us to reach our present level of development – and that's a tremendous length of time! Almost all the progress we've made has been due to our telepathic powers: without them we'd be little different from all those other animals that show such puzzling resemblances to us. We're very proud of our philosophy and our mathematics, of our music and dancing – but have you ever thought, Eris, that there might be other lines of cultural development which we've never even dreamed of? *That there might be other forces in the Universe beside mental ones*?'

'I don't know what you mean,' said Eris flatly.

'It's hard to explain, and I won't try – except to say this. Do you realize just how pitiably feeble is our control over the external world, and how useless these limbs of ours really are? No – you can't, for you won't have seen what I have. But perhaps this will make you understand.'

The pattern of Aretenon's thoughts modulated suddenly into a minor key.

'I remember once coming upon a bank of beautiful and curiously complicated flowers. I wanted to see what they were like inside, so I tried to open one, steadying it between my hooves and picking it apart with my teeth. I tried again and again – and failed. In the end, half mad with rage, I trampled all those flowers into the dirt.'

Jeryl could detect the perplexity in Eris's mind, but she could see that he was interested and curious to know more.

'I have had that sort of feeling, too,' he admitted. 'But what can one do about it? And after all, is it really important? There are a good many things in this universe which are not exactly as we should like them.'

Aretenon smiled.

'That's true enough. But Therodimus has found how to do something about it. Will you come and see him?'

'It must be a long journey.'

'About twenty days from here, and we have to go across a river.'

Jeryl felt Eris give a little shudder. The Atheleni hated water, for the excellent and sufficient reason that they were too heavily boned to swim, and promptly drowned if they fell into it.

'It's in enemy territory: they won't like me.'

'They respect you, and it might be a good idea for you to go – a friendly gesture, as it were.'

'But I'm wanted here.'

'You can take my word that nothing you do here is as important as the message Therodimus has for you – and for the whole world.'

Eris veiled his thoughts for a moment, then uncovered them briefly.

'I'll think about it,' he said.

It was surprising how little Aretenon managed to say on the many days of the journey. From time to time Eris would challenge the defences of his mind with half-playful thrusts, but always they were parried with an effortless skill. About the ultimate weapon that had ended the War he would say nothing, but Eris knew that those who had wielded it had not yet disbanded and were still at their secret hiding-place. Yet though he would not talk about the past, Aretenon often spoke of the future, and with the urgent anxiety of one who had helped to shape it and was not sure if he had acted aright. Like many others of his race, he was haunted by what he had done, and the sense of guilt sometimes overwhelmed him. Often he made remarks which puzzled Eris at the time, but which he was to remember more and more vividly in the years ahead.

'We've come to a turning-point in our history, Eris. The powers we've uncovered will soon be shared by the Mithraneans, and another war will mean destruction for us both. All my life I've worked to increase our knowledge of the mind, but now I wonder if I've brought something into the world that is too powerful, and too dangerous for us to handle. Yet it's too late, now, to retrace our footsteps: sooner or later our culture was bound to come to this point, and to discover what we have found.

'It's a terrible dilemma: and there's only one solution. We cannot go back, and if we go forward we may meet disaster. So we must change the very nature of our civilization, and break completely with the million generations behind us. You can't imagine how that could be done: nor could I, until I met Therodimus and he told me of his dream.

'The mind is a wonderful thing, Eris – but by itself it is helpless in the universe of matter. We know now how to multiply the power of our brains by an enormous factor: we can solve, perhaps, the great problems of mathematics that have baffled us for ages. But neither our unaided minds, nor the group-mind we've now created, can alter in the slightest the one fact that all through history has brought us and the Mithraneans into conflict – the fact that the food supply is fixed, and our populations are not.'

Jeryl would watch them, taking little part in their thoughts, as they argued these matters. Most of their discussions took place while they were browsing, for like all active ruminants they had to spend a considerable part of each day searching for food. Fortunately the land through which they were passing was extremely fertile – indeed, its fertility had been one of the causes of the War. Eris, Jeryl was glad to see, was becoming something of his old self again. The feeling of frustrated bitterness that had filled his mind for so many months had not lifted, but it was no longer as all-pervading as it had been.

They left the open plain on the twenty-second day of their journey. For a long time they had been travelling through Mithranean territory, but those few of their ex-enemies they had seen had been inquisitive rather than hostile. Now the grasslands were coming to an end, and the forest with all its primeval terrors lay ahead.

'Only one carnivore lives in this region,' Aretenon reassured them, 'and it's no match for the three of us. We'll be past the trees in a day and a night.'

'A night – in the forest!' gasped Jeryl, half-petrified with terror at the very thought.

Aretenon was obviously a little ashamed of himself.

'I didn't like to mention it before,' he apologized, 'but there's really no danger. I've done it by myself, several times. After all, none of the great flesh-eaters of ancient times still exists – and it won't be really dark, even in the woods. The red sun will still be up.'

Jeryl was still trembling slightly. She came of a race which, for thousands of generations, had lived on the high hills and the open plains, relying on speed to escape from danger. The thought of going among trees – and in the dim red twilight while the primary sun was down – filled her with panic. And of the three of them, only Aretenon possessed a horn with which to fight. (It was nothing like so long or sharp, thought Jeryl, as Eris's had been.)

She was still not at all happy even when they had spent a completely uneventful day moving through the woods. The only animals they saw were tiny, long-tailed creatures that ran up and down the tree-trunks with amazing speed, gibbering with anger as the intruders passed. It was entertaining to watch them, but Jeryl did not think that the forest would be quite so amusing in the night.

Her fears were well founded. When the fierce white sun passed below the trees, and the crimson shadows of the red giant lay everywhere, a change seemed to come over the world. A sudden silence swept across the forest – a silence abruptly broken by a very distant wail towards which the three of them turned instinctively, ancestral warnings shrieking in their minds.

'What was that?' gasped Jeryl.

Aretenon was breathing swiftly, but his reply was calm enough.

'Never mind,' he said. 'It was a long way off. I don't know what it was.'

They took turns to keep guard, and the long night wore slowly away. From time to time Jeryl would awaken from troubled dreams into the nightmare reality of the strange, distorted trees gathered threateningly around her. Once, when she was on guard, she heard the sound of a heavy body moving through the woods very far away – but it came no nearer and she did not disturb the others. So at last the longed-for brilliance of the white sun began to flood the sky, and the day had come again.

Aretenon, Jeryl thought, was probably more relieved than he pretended to be. He was almost boyish as he frisked around in the morning sunlight, snatching an occasional mouthful of foliage from an overhanging branch.

'We've only half a day to go now,' he said cheerfully. 'We'll be out of the forest by noon.'

There was a mischievous undertone to his thoughts that puzzled Jeryl. It seemed as if Aretenon was keeping still another secret from them, and Jeryl wondered what further obstacles they would have to overcome. By mid-day she knew, for their way was barred by a great river flowing slowly past them as if in no haste to meet the sea.

Eris looked at it with some annoyance, measuring it with a practised eye.

'It's much too deep to ford here. We'll have to go a long way upstream before we can cross.'

Aretenon smiled.

'On the contrary,' he said cheerfully, 'we're going *downstream*.'

Eris and Jeryl looked at him in amazement.

'Are you mad?' Eris cried.

'You'll soon see. We've not far to go now – you've come all this way, so you might as well trust me for the rest of the journey.'

The river slowly widened and deepened. If it had been impassable before, it was doubly so now. Sometimes, Eris knew, one came upon a stream across which a tree had fallen, so that one could walk over the trunk – though it was a risky thing to do. But this river was the width of many trees, and was growing no narrower.

'We're nearly there,' said Aretenon at last. 'I recognize the place. Someone should be coming out of those woods at any moment.' He gestured with his horn to the trees on the far side of the river, and almost as he did so three figures came bounding out on to the bank. Two of them, Jeryl saw, were Atheleni: the third was a Mithranean.

They were now nearing a great tree, standing by the water's edge, but Jeryl had paid little attention: she was too interested in the figures on the distant bank, wondering what they were going to do next. So when Eris's amazement exploded like a thunderclap in the depths of her own mind, she was too confused for a moment to realize its cause. Then she turned towards the tree, and saw what Eris had seen.

To some minds and some races, few things could have been more natural or more commonplace than a thick rope tied round a tree-trunk, and floating out across the water of a river to another tree on the far bank. Yet it filled both Jeryl and Eris with the terror of the unknown, and for one awful moment Jeryl thought that a gigantic snake was emerging from the water. Then she saw that it was not alive, but her fear remained. For it was the first artificial object that she had ever seen.

'Don't worry about *what* it is, or how it was put there,' counselled Aretenon. 'It's going to carry you across, and that's all that matters for the moment. Look – there's someone coming over now!'

One of the figures on the far bank had lowered itself into the water, and was working its way with its forelimbs along the rope. As it came nearer – it was the Mithranean, and a female – Jeryl saw that it was carrying a second and much smaller rope looped round the upper part of its body.

With the skill of long practice, the stranger made her way across the floating cable, and emerged dripping from the river. She seemed to know Aretenon, but Jeryl could not intercept their thoughts.

'I can go across without any help,' said Aretenon, 'but I'll show you the easy way.'

He slipped the loop over his shoulders, and, dropping into the water, hooked his forelimbs over the fixed cable. A moment later he was being dragged across at a great speed by the two others on the far bank, where, after much trepidation, Eris and Jeryl presently joined him.

It was not the sort of bridge one would expect from a race

which could quite easily have dealt with the mathematics of a reinforced concrete arch – if the possibility of such an object had ever occurred to it. But it served its purpose, and once it had been made, they could use it readily enough.

Once it had been made. But – who had made it?

When their dripping guides had rejoined them, Aretenon gave his friends a warning.

'I'm afraid you're going to have a good many shocks while you're here. You'll see some very strange sights, but when you understand them, they'll cease to puzzle you in the slightest. In fact, you will soon come to take them for granted.'

One of the strangers, whose thoughts neither Eris nor Jeryl could intercept, was giving him a message.

'Therodimus is waiting for us,' said Aretenon. 'He's very anxious to see you.'

'I've been trying to contact him,' complained Eris, 'but I've not succeeded.'

Aretenon seemed a little troubled.

'You'll find he's changed,' he said. 'After all, you've not seen each other for many years. It may be some time before you can make full contact again.'

Their road was a winding one through the forest, and from time to time curiously narrow paths branched off in various directions. Therodimus, thought Eris, must have changed indeed for him to have taken up permanent residence among trees. Presently the track opened out into a large, semicircular clearing with a low white cliff lying along its diameter. At the foot of the cliff were several dark holes of varying sizes – obviously the openings of caves.

It was the first time that either Eris or Jeryl had ever entered a cave, and they did not greatly look forward to the experience. They were relieved when Aretenon told them to wait just outside the opening, and went on alone towards the puzzling yellow light that glowed in the depths.

A moment later, dim memories began to pulse in Eris's mind, and he knew that his old teacher was coming, even though he could no longer fully share his thoughts.

Something stirred in the gloom, and then Therodimus came out into the sunlight. At the sight of him, Jeryl screamed once and buried her head in Eris's mane, but Eris stood firm, though he was trembling as he had never done before battle. For Therodimus blazed with a magnificence that none of his race had ever known since history began. Around his neck hung a band of glittering objects that caught and refracted the sunlight in myriad colours, while covering his body was a sheet of some thick, many-hued material that rustled softly as he walked. And his horn was no longer the yellow of ivory: some magic had changed it to the most wonderful purple that Jeryl had ever seen.

Therodimus stood motionless for a moment, savouring their amazement to the full. Then his rich laugh echoed in their minds, and he reared up on his hind limb. The coloured garment fell whispering to the ground, and at a toss of his head the glittering necklace arched like a rainbow into a corner of the cave. But the purple horn remained unchanged.

It seemed to Eris that he stood at the brink of a great chasm, with Therodimus beckoning him on the far side. Their thoughts struggled to form a bridge, but could make no contact. Between them was the gulf of half a lifetime and many battles, of a myriad unshared experiences – Therodimus's years in this strange land, his own mating with Jeryl and the memory of their lost children. Though they stood face to face, a few feet only between them, their thoughts could never meet again.

Then Aretenon, with all the power and authority of his unsurpassed skill, did something to his mind that Eris was never quite able to recall. He only knew that the years seemed to have rolled back, that he was once more the eager, anxious pupil – and that he could speak to Therodimus again.

It was strange to sleep underground, but less unpleasant than spending the night amid the unknown terrors of the forest. As she watched the crimson shadows deepening beyond the entrance to the little cave, Jeryl tried to collect her scattered thoughts. She had understood only a small part of what had passed between Eris and Therodimus, but she knew that something incredible was taking place. The evidence of her eyes was enough to prove that: today she had seen things for which there were no words in her language.

She had heard things, too. As they had passed one of the cave-mouths, there had come from it a rhythmic 'whirring' sound, unlike that made by any animal she knew. It had continued steadily without pause or break as long as she could hear it, and even now its unhurried rhythm had not left her mind. Aretenon, she believed, had also noticed it, though without any surprise: Eris had been so engrossed with Therodimus.

The old philosopher had told them very little, preferring, as he said, to show them his empire when they had had a good night's rest. Nearly all their talk had been concerned with the events of their own land during the last few years, and Jeryl found it somewhat boring. Only one thing had interested her, and she had eyes for little else. That was the wonderful chain of coloured crystals that Therodimus had worn around his neck. What it was, or how it had been created, she could not imagine: but she coveted it. As she fell asleep, she found herself thinking idly, but more than half-seriously, of the sensation it would cause if she returned to her people with such a marvel gleaming against her own pelt. It would look so much better there than upon old Therodimus.

Aretenon and Therodimus met them at the cave soon after dawn. The philosopher had discarded his regalia – which he had obviously worn only to impress his guests – and his horn had returned to its normal yellow. That was one thing Jeryl thought she could understand, for she had come across fruits whose juices could cause colour changes.

Therodimus settled himself at the mouth of the cave. He began his narration without preliminaries, and Eris guessed that he must have told it many times before to earlier visitors.

'I came to this place, Eris, about five years after leaving our country. As you know, I was always interested in strange lands, and from the Mithraneans I'd heard rumours that intrigued me very much. How I traced them to their source is a long story that doesn't matter now. I crossed the river far upstream one summer, when the water was very low. There's only one place where it can be done, and then only in the driest years. Higher still the river loses itself in the mountains, and I don't think there's any way through them. So this is virtually an island – almost completely cut off from Mithranean territory.

'It's an island, but it's not uninhabited. The people who live here are called the Phileni, and they have a very re-markable culture – one entirely different from our own. Some of the products of that culture you've already seen.

'As you know, there are many different races on our world, and quite a few of them have some sort of intelli-gence. But there is a great gulf between us and all other creatures. As far as we know, we are the only beings capable of abstract thought and complex logical processes.

'The Phileni are a much younger race than ours, and they are intermediate between us and the other animals. They've lived here on this rather large island for several thousand generations – but their rate of development has been many, many times swifter than ours. They neither possess nor understand our telepathic powers, but they have something else which we may well envy – something which is responsible for the whole of their civilization and its incredibly rapid progress.'

Therodimus paused, then rose slowly to his feet.

'Follow me,' he said. 'I'll take you to see the Phileni.'

He led them back to the caves from which they had come the night before, pausing at the entrance from which Jeryl had heard that strange, rhythmic whirring. It was clearer and louder now, and she saw Eris start as though he had noticed it for the first time. Then Therodimus uttered a high-pitched whistle, and at once the whirring slackened, falling octave by octave until it had ebbed into silence. A moment later something came towards them out of the semi-gloom.

It was a little creature, scarcely half their height, and it did not hop, but walked upon two jointed limbs that seemed very thin and feeble. Its large spherical head was dominated by three huge eyes, set far apart and capable of independent movement. With the best will in the world, Jeryl did not think it was very attractive.

Then Therodimus uttered another whistle, and the creature raised its forelimbs towards them.

'Look closely,' said Therodimus, very gently, 'and you will see the answer to many of your questions.'

For the first time, Jeryl saw that the creature's forelimbs did not end in hooves, or indeed after the fashion of any animal with which she was acquainted. Instead, they divided into at least a dozen thin, flexible tentacles and two hooked claws.

'Go towards it, Jeryl,' commanded Therodimus. 'It has something for you.'

Hesitantly, Jeryl moved forward. She noticed that the creature's body was crossed with bands of dark material, to which were attached unidentifiable objects. It dropped a forelimb to one of these, and a cover opened to reveal a cavity inside which something glittered. Then the little tentacles were clutching that marvellous crystal necklace, and with a movement so swift and dexterous that Jeryl could scarcely follow it, the Phileni moved forward and clasped it round her neck.

Therodimus brushed aside her confusion and gratitude, but his shrewd old mind was well pleased. Jeryl would be his ally now in whatever he planned to do. But Eris's emotions might not be so easily swayed, and in this matter mere logic was not enough. His old pupil had changed so much, had been so deeply wounded by the past, that Therodimus could not be certain of success. Yet he had a plan that could turn even these difficulties to his advantage.

He gave another whistle, and the Phileni made a curious waving gesture with its hands and disappeared into the cave. A moment later that strange whirring ascended once more from the silence, but Jeryl's curiosity was now quite over-shadowed by her delight in her new possession.

'We'll go through the woods,' said Therodimus, 'to the nearest settlement – it's only a little way from here. The Phileni don't live in the open, as we do. In fact, they differ from us in almost every conceivable way. I'm even afraid,' he added ruefully, 'that they're much better natured than we are, and I believe that one day they'll be more intelligent. But first of all, let me tell you what I've learned about them, so that you can understand what I'm planning to do.'

The mental evolution of any race is conditioned, even dominated, by physical factors which that race almost invariably takes for granted as part of the natural order of things. The wonderfully sensitive hands of the Phileni had enabled them to find by experiment and trial facts which had taken the planet's only other intelligent species a thousand times as long to discover by pure deduction. Quite

96

early in their history, the Phileni had invented simple tools. From these they had proceeded to fabrics, pottery, and the use of fire. When Therodimus had discovered them, they had already invented the lathe and the potter's wheel, and were about to move into their first Metal Age – with all that that implied.

On the purely intellectual plane, their progress had been less rapid. They were clever and skilled, but they had a dislike of abstract thought and their mathematics was purely empirical. They knew, for example, that a triangle with sides in the ratio three-four-five was right-angled, but had not suspected that this was only a special case of a much more general law. Their knowledge was full of such yawning gaps, which, despite the help of Therodimus and his several score disciples, they seemed in no great hurry to fill.

Therodimus they worshipped as a god, and for two whole generations of their short-lived race they had obeyed him in everything, giving him all the products of their skill that he needed, and making at his suggestion the new tools and devices that had occurred to him. The partnership had been incredibly fertile, for it was as if both races had suddenly been released from their shackles. Great manual skill and great intellectual powers had fused in a fruitful union probably unique in all the universe – and progress that would normally have taken millennia had been achieved in less than a decade.

As Aretenon had promised them, though Eris and Jeryl saw many marvels, they came across nothing that they could not understand once they had watched the little Phileni craftsmen at work and had seen with what magic their hands shaped natural materials into lovely or useful forms. Even their tiny towns and primitive farms soon lost their wonder and became part of the accepted order of things.

Therodimus let them look their fill, until they had seen every aspect of this strangely sophisticated Stone Age culture. Because they knew no differently, they found nothing incongruous in the sight of a Phileni potter – who could scarcely count beyond ten – shaping a series of complex algebraic surfaces under the guidance of a young Mithranean mathematician. Like all his race, Eris possessed tremendous powers of mental visualization, but he realized how much easier geometry would be if one could actually *see* the shapes one was considering. From this beginning (though he could not guess it) would one day evolve the idea of a written language.

Jeryl was fascinated above all things by the sight of the little Phileni women weaving fabrics upon their primitive looms. She could sit for hours watching the flying shuttles and wishing that she could use them. Once one had seen it done, it seemed so simple and obvious – and so utterly beyond the powers of the clumsy, useless limbs of her own people.

They grew very fond of the Phileni, who seemed eager to please and were pathetically proud of all their manual skills. In these new and novel surroundings, meeting fresh wonders every day, Eris seemed to be recovering from some of the scars which the War had left upon his mind. Jeryl knew, however, that there was still much damage to be undone. Sometimes, before he could hide them, she would come across raw, angry wounds in the depths of Eris's mind, and she feared that many of them – like the broken stump of his horn – would never heal. Eris had hated the War, and the manner of its ending still oppressed him. Beyond this, Jeryl knew, he was haunted by the fear that it might come again.

These troubles she often discussed with Therodimus, of whom she had now grown very fond. She still did not fully understand why he had brought them here, or what he and his followers were planning to do. Therodimus was in no hurry to explain his actions, for he wished Jeryl and Eris to draw their own conclusions as far as possible. But at last, five days after their arrival, he called them to his cave.

'You've now seen,' he began, 'most of the things we have to show you here. You know what the Phileni can do, and perhaps you have thought how much our own lives will be enriched once we can use the products of their skill. That was my first thought when I came here, all those years ago.

'It was an obvious and rather naïve idea, but it led to a much greater one. As I grew to know the Phileni, and found how swiftly their minds had advanced in so short a time, I realized what a fearful disadvantage our own race had always laboured under. I began to wonder how much further forward *we* would have been had we the Phileni's control over the physical world. It is not a question of mere convenience, or the ability to make beautiful things like that necklace of yours, Jeryl, but something much more profound. It is the difference between ignorance and knowledge, between weakness and power.

'We have developed our minds, and our minds alone, until we can go no further. As Aretenon has told you, we have now come to a danger that threatens our entire race. We are under the shadow of the irresistible weapon against which there can be no defence.

'The solution is, quite literally, in the hands of the Phileni. We must use their skills to reshape our world, and so remove the cause of all our wars. We must go back to the beginning and re-lay the foundations of our culture. It won't be *our* culture alone, though, for we shall share it with the Phileni. They will be the hands – we the brains. Oh, I have dreamed of the world that may come, ages ahead, when even the marvels you see around you now will be considered childish toys! But not many are philosophers, and I need an argument more substantial than dreams. That final argument I believe I may have found, though I cannot yet be certain.

'I have asked you here, Eris, partly because I wanted to renew our old friendship, and partly because your word will now have far greater influence than mine. You are a hero among your own people, and the Mithraneans also will listen to you. I want you to return, taking with you some of the Phileni and their products. Show them to your people, and ask them to send their young men here to help us with our work.'

There was a pause during which Jeryl could gather no hints of Eris's thoughts. Then he replied hesitantly:

'But I still don't understand. These things that the Phileni make are very pretty, and some of them may be useful to us. But how can they change us as profoundly as you seem to think?'

Therodimus sighed. Eris could not see past the present into the future that was yet to be. He had not caught, as Therodimus had done, the promise that lay beyond the busy hands and tools of the Phileni – the first faint possibilities of the Machine. Perhaps he would never understand: but he could still be convinced.

Veiling his deeper thoughts, Therodimus continued:

'Perhaps some of these things are toys, Eris – but they may be more powerful than you think. Jeryl, I know, would be loath to part with hers ... and perhaps I can find one that would convince you.'

Eris was sceptical, and Jeryl could see that he was in one of his darker moods.

'I doubt it very much,' he said.

'Well, I can try.' Therodimus gave a whistle, and one of the Phileni came running up. There was a short exchange of conversation.

'Would you come with me Eris? It will take some time.'

Eris followed him, the others, at Therodimus's request, remaining behind. They left the large cave and went towards the row of smaller ones which the Phileni used for their various trades.

The strange whirring noise was sounding loudly in Eris's ears, but for a moment he could not see its cause, the light of the crude oil lamps being too faint for his eyes. Then he made out one of the Phileni bending over a wooden table upon which something was spinning rapidly, driven by a belt from a treadle operated by another of the little creatures. He had seen the potters using a similar device, but this was different. It was shaping wood, not clay, and the potter's fingers had been replaced by a sharp metal blade from which long, thin shavings were curling out in fascinating spirals. With their huge eyes the Phileni, who disliked full sunlight, could see perfectly in the gloom, but it was some time before Eris could discover just what was happening. Then suddenly, he understood.

'Aretenon,' said Jeryl when the others had left them, 'why should the Phileni do all these things for us? Surely they're quite happy as they are?'

The question, Aretenon thought was typical of Jeryl and would never have been asked by Eris.

'They will do anything that Therodimus says,' he answered, 'but even apart from that there's so much we can give them as well. When we turn our minds to their problems, we can see how to solve them in ways that would never have occurred to them. They're very eager to learn, and already we must have advanced their culture by hundreds of generations. Also, they're physically very feeble. Although we don't possess their dexterity, our strength makes possible tasks they could never attempt.'

They had wandered to the edge of the river, and stood for

a moment watching the unhurried waters moving down to the sea. Then Jeryl turned to go upstream, but Aretenon stopped her.

'Therodimus doesn't want us to go that way, yet,' he explained. 'It's just another of his little secrets. He never likes to reveal his plans until they're ready.'

Slightly piqued, and distinctly curious, Jeryl obediently turned back. She would, of course, come this way again as soon as there was no one else about.

It was very peaceful here in the warm sunlight, among the pools of heat trapped by the trees. Jeryl had almost lost her fear of the forest, though she knew she would never be quite happy there.

Aretenon seemed very abstracted, and Jeryl knew that he wished to say something and was marshalling his thoughts. Presently he began to speak, with the freedom that is only possible between two people who are fond of each other but have no emotional ties.

'It is very hard, Jeryl,' he began, 'to turn one's back on the work of a lifetime. Once I had hoped that the great new forces we have discovered could be safely used, but now I know that it is impossible, at least for many ages. Therodimus was right – we can go no further with our minds alone. Our culture has been hopelessly one-sided, though through no fault of ours. We cannot solve the fundamental problem of peace and war without a command over the physical world such as the Phileni possess – and which we hope to borrow from them.

'Perhaps there will be other great adventures here for our minds, to make us forget what we will have to abandon. We shall be able to learn something from Nature at last. What is the difference between fire and water, between wood and stone? What are the suns, and what are those millions of faint lights we see in the sky when both the suns are down? Perhaps the answers to all these questions may lie at the end of the new road along which we must travel.'

He paused.

'New knowledge – new wisdom – in realms we have never dreamed of before. It may lure us away from the dangers we have encountered: for certainly nothing we can learn from Nature will ever be as great a threat as the peril we have uncovered in our own minds.'

The flow of Aretenon's thoughts was suddenly interrupted. Then he said: 'I think Eris wants to see you.'

Jeryl wondered why Eris had not sent the message to her: she wondered, too, at the undertone of amusement – or was it something else? – in Aretenon's mind.

There was no sign of Eris as they approached the caves, but he was waiting for them and came bounding out into the sunlight before they could reach the entrance. Then Jeryl gave an involuntary cry, and retreated a pace or two as her mate came towards her.

For Eris was whole again. Gone was the shattered stump on his forehead: it had been replaced by a new, gleaming horn no less splendid than the one he had lost.

In a belated gesture of greeting, Eris touched horns with Aretenon. Then he was gone into the forest in great joyous leaps – but not before his mind had met Jeryl's as it had seldom done since the days before the War.

'Let him go,' said Therodimus softly. 'He would rather be alone. When he returns I think you will find him – different.' He gave a laugh. 'The Phileni are clever, are they not? Now, perhaps, Eris will be more appreciative of their "toys".'

'I know I am impatient,' said Therodimus, 'but I am old now, and I want to see the changes begin in my own lifetime. That is why I am starting so many schemes in the hope that some at least will succeed. But this is the one, above all, in which I have put most faith.'

103

For a moment he lost himself in his thoughts. Not one in a hundred of his own race could fully share his dream. Even Eris, though he now believed in it, did so with his heart rather than his mind. Perhaps Aretenon – the brilliant and subtle Aretenon, so desperately anxious to neutralize the powers he had brought into the world – might have glimpsed the reality. But his was of all minds the most impenetrable, save when he wished otherwise.

'You know as well as I do,' continued Therodimus, as they walked upstream, 'that our wars have only one cause – Food. We and the Mithraneans are trapped on this continent of ours with its limited resources, which we can do nothing to increase. Ahead of us we have always the nightmare of starvation, and for all our vaunted intelligence there has been nothing we can do about it. Oh yes, we have scraped some laborious irrigation ditches with our fore-hooves, but how slight their help has been!

'The Phileni have discovered how to grow crops that increase the fertility of the ground manyfold. I believe that we can do the same – once we have adapted their tools for our own use. That is our first and most important task, but it is not the one on which I have set my heart. The final solution to our problem, Eris, *must be the discovery of new, virgin lands into which our people can migrate.*'

He smiled at the other's amazement.

'No, don't think I'm mad. Such lands do exist, I'm sure of it. Once I stood at the edge of the ocean and watched a great flight of birds coming inland from far out at sea. I have seen them flying outwards, too, so purposefully that I was certain they were going to some other country. And I have followed them with my thoughts.'

'Even if your theory is true, as it probably is,' said Eris, 'what use is it to us?' he gestured to the river flowing beside them. 'We drown in the water, and you cannot build a rope to support us —' His thoughts suddenly faded out into a

104

jumbled chaos of ideas.

Therodimus smiled.

'So you have guessed what I hope to do. Well, now you can see if you are right.'

They had come to a level stretch of bank, upon which a group of the Phileni were busily as work, under the supervision of some of Therodimus's assistants. Lying at the water's edge was a strange object which, Eris realized, was made of many tree-trunks joined together by ropes.

They watched in fascination as the orderly tumult reached its climax. There was a great pulling and pushing, and the raft moved ponderously into the water with a mighty splash. The spray had scarcely ceased to fall when a young Mithranean leaped from the bank and began to dance gleefully upon the logs, which were now tugging at the moorings as if eager to break away and follow the river down to the sea. A moment later he had been joined by others, rejoicing in their mastery of a new element. The little Phileni, unable to make the leap, stood watching patiently on the bank while their masters enjoyed themselves.

There was an exhilaration about the scene that no one could fail to miss, though perhaps few of those present realized that they were at a turning-point in history. Only Therodimus stood a little apart from the rest, lost in his own thoughts. This primitive raft, he knew, was merely a beginning. It must be tested upon the river, then along the shores of the ocean. The work would take years, and he was never likely to see the first voyagers returning from those fabulous lands whose existence was still no more than a guess. But what had been begun, others would finish.

Overhead, a flight of birds was passing across the forest, Therodimus watched them go, envying their freedom to move at will over land and sea. He had begun the conquest of the water for his race, but that the skies might one day be theirs also was beyond even his imagination.

Aretenon, Jeryl and the rest of the expedition had already crossed the river when Eris said good-bye to Therodimus. This time they had done so without a drop of water touching their bodies, for the raft had come downstream and was performing valuable duties as a ferry. A new and much improved model was already under construction, as it was painfully obvious that the prototype was not exactly seaworthy. These initial difficulties would be quickly overcome by designers who, even if they were forced to work with Stone Age tools, could handle with ease the mathematics of metacentres, buoyancies and advanced hydrodynamics.

'Your task won't be a simple one,' said Therodimus, 'for you cannot show your people all the things you have seen here. At first you must be content to sow the seed, to arouse interest and curiosity – particularly among the young, who will come here to learn more. Perhaps you will meet opposition: I expect so. But every time you return to us, we shall have new things to show you and to strengthen your arguments.'

They touched horns: then Eris was gone, taking with him the knowledge that was to change the world – so slowly at first, then ever more swiftly. Once the barriers were down, once the Mithraneans and the Atheleni had been given the simple tools which they could fasten to their forelimbs and use unaided, progress would be swift. But for the present they must rely on the Phileni for everything: and there were so few of them.

Therodimus was well content. Only in one respect was he disappointed, for he had hoped that Eris, who had always been his favourite, might also be his successor. The Eris who was now returning to his own people was no longer self-obsessed or embittered, for he had a mission and hope for the future. But he lacked the keen, far-ranging vision that was needed here: it would be Aretenon who must continue what he had begun. Still, that could not be helped, and there was no need yet to think of such matters. Therodimus was very old, but he knew that he would be meeting Eris many times again here by the river at the entrance to his land.

The ferry was gone now, and though he had expected it, Eris stopped amazed at the great span of the bridge, swaying slightly in the breeze. Its execution did not quite match its design – a good deal of mathematics had gone into its parabolic suspension – but it was still the first great engineering feat in history. Constructed though it was entirely of wood and rope, it forecast the shape of the metal giants to come.

Eris paused in mid-stream. He could see smoke rising from the shipyards facing the ocean, and thought he could just glimpse the masts of some of the new vessels that were being built for coastal trade. It was hard to believe that when he had first crossed this river he had been dragged over dangling from a rope.

Aretenon was waiting for them on the far bank. He moved rather slowly now, but his eyes were still bright with the old, eager intelligence. He greeted Eris warmly.

'I'm glad you could come now. You're just in time.'

That, Eris knew, could mean only one thing.

'The ships are back?'

'Almost: they were sighted an hour ago out on the horizon. They should be here at any moment, and then we shall know the truth at last, after all these years. If only —'

His thoughts faded out, but Eris could continue them. They had come to the great pyramid of stones beneath which Therodimus lay – Therodimus, whose brain was behind everything they saw, but who could never learn now if his most cherished dream was true or not.

There was a storm coming up from the ocean, and they

hurried along the new road that skirted the river's edge. Small boats of a kind that Eris had not seen before went past them occasionally, operated by Atheleni or Mithraneans with wooden paddles strapped to their forelimbs. It always gave Eris great pleasure to see such new conquests, such new liberations of his people from their age-old chains. Yet sometimes they reminded him of children who had suddenly been let loose into a wonderful new world, full of exciting and interesting things that must be done, whether they were likely to be useful or not. However, anything that promised to make his race into better sailors was more than useful. In the last decade Eris had discovered that pure intelligence was sometimes not enough: there were skills that could not be acquired by any amount of mental effort. Though his people had largely overcome their fear of water, they were still quite incompetent on the ocean, and the Phileni had therefore become the first navigators of the world.

Jeryl looked nervously around her as the first peal of thunder came rolling in from the sea. She was still wearing the necklace that Therodimus had given her so long ago: but it was by no means the only ornament she carried now.

'I hope the ships will be safe,' she said anxiously.

'There's not much wind, and they will have ridden out much worse storms than this,' Aretenon reassured her, as they entered his cave. Eris and Jeryl looked round with eager interest to see what new wonders the Phileni had made during their absence: but if there were any they had, as usual, been hidden away until Aretenon was ready to show them. He was still rather childishly fond of such little surprises and mysteries.

There was an air of absentmindedness about the meeting that would have puzzled an onlooker ignorant of its cause. As Eris talked of all the changes in the outer world, of the success of the new Phileni settlements, and of the steady growth of agriculture among his people, Aretenon listened with only half his mind. His thoughts, and those of his friends, were far out at sea, meeting the oncoming ships which might be bringing the greatest news their world had ever received.

As Eris finished his report, Aretenon got up and began to move restlessly around the chamber.

'You have done better than we dared to hope at the beginning. At least there has been no war for a generation, and our food supply is ahead of the population for the first time in history – thanks to our new agricultural techniques.'

Aretenon glanced at the furnishings of his chamber, recalling with an effort the fact that in his own youth almost everything he saw would have appeared impossible or even meaningless to him. Not even the simplest of tools had existed then, at least in the knowledge of his people. Now there were ships and bridges and houses – and these were only the beginning.

'I am well satisfied,' he said. 'We have, as we planned, diverted the whole stream of our culture, turning it away from the dangers that lay ahead. The powers that made the Madness possible will soon be forgotten : only a handful of us still know of them, and we will take our secrets with us. Perhaps when our descendants rediscover them they will be wise enough to use them properly. But we have uncovered so many new wonders that it may be a thousand generations before we turn again to look into our own minds and to tamper with the forces locked within them.'

The mouth of the cave was illuminated by a sudden flash of lightning. The storm was coming nearer, though it was still some miles away. Rain was beginning to fall in large, angry drops from the leaden sky.

'While we're waiting for the ships,' said Aretenon rather abruptly, 'come into the next cave and see some of the new things we have to show you since your last visit.'

109

It was a strange collection. Side by side on the same bench were tools and inventions which in other cultures had been separated by thousands of years of time. The Stone Age was past: bronze and iron had come, and already the first crude scientific instruments had been built for experiments that were driving back the frontiers of the unknown. A primitive retort spoke of the beginnings of chemistry, and by its side were the first lenses the world had seen – waiting to reveal the unsuspected universes of the infinitely small and the infinitely great.

The storm was upon them as Aretenon's description of these new wonders drew to its close. From time to time he had glanced nervously at the mouth of the cave, as if awaiting a messenger from the harbour, but they had remained undisturbed save by the occasional crash of thunder.

'I've shown you everything of importance,' he said, 'but here's something that may amuse you while we're waiting. As I said, we've sent expeditions everywhere to collect and classify all the rocks they can, in the hope of finding useful minerals. One of them brought back this.'

He extinguished the lights and the cave became completely dark.

'It will be some time before your eyes grow sensitive enough to see it,' Aretenon warned. 'Just look over there in that corner.'

Eris strained his eyes into the darkness. At first he could see nothing: then, slowly, a glimmering blue light became faintly visible. It was so vague and diffuse that he could not focus his eyes upon it, and he automatically moved forward.

'I shouldn't go too near,' advised Aretenon. 'It seems to be a perfectly ordinary mineral, but the Phileni who found it and carried it here got some very strange burns from handling it. Yet it's quite cold to the touch. One day we'll learn its secret: but I don't suppose it's anything at all important.'

A vast curtain of sheet lightning split the sky, and for a

moment the reflected glare lit up the cave, pinning weird shadows against the walls. At the same moment one of the Phileni staggered into the entrance and called something to Aretenon in its thin, reedy voice. He gave a great shout of triumph as one of his ancestors might have done on some ancient battlefield: then his thoughts came crashing into Eris's mind.

'Land! They've found land – a whole new continent waiting for us!'

Eris felt the sense of triumph and victory well up within him like water bursting from a spring. Clear ahead now into the future lay the new, the glorious road along which their children would travel, mastering the world and all its secrets as they went. The vision of Therodimus was at last sharp and brilliant before his eyes.

He felt for the mind of Jeryl, so that she could share his joy – and found that it was closed to him. Leaning towards her in the darkness, he could sense that she was still staring into the depths of the cave, as if she had never heard the wonderful news, and could not tear her eyes away from that enigmatic glow.

Out of the night came the roar of the belated thunder as it raced across the sky. Eris felt Jeryl tremble beside him, and sent out his thoughts to comfort her.

'Don't let the thunder frighten you,' he said gently. 'What is there to fear now?'

'I do not know,' replied Jeryl. 'I am frightened – but not of the thunder. Oh, Eris, it is a wonderful thing we have done, and I wish Therodimus could be here to see it. But where will it lead in the end – this new road of ours?'

Out of the past, the words that Aretenon had once spoken had risen to haunt her. She remembered their walk by the river, long ago, when he had talked of his hopes and had said: 'Certainly nothing we can learn from Nature will ever be as great a threat as the peril we have encountered in our

111

own minds.' Now the words seemed to mock her and to cast a shadow over the golden future: but why, she could not say.

Alone, perhaps, of all the races in the Universe, her people had reached the second cross-roads – and had never passed the first. Now they must go along the road that they had missed, and must face the challenge at its end – the challenge from which, this time, they could not escape.

In the darkness, the faint glow of dying atoms burned unwavering in the rock. It would still be burning there, scarcely dimmed, when Jeryl and Eris had been dust for centuries. It would be only a little fainter when the civilization they were building had at last unlocked its secrets.

THE SENTINEL

THE next time you see the full Moon high in the south, look carefully at its right-hand edge and let your eye travel upwards along the curve of the disc. Round about two o'clock, you will notice a small, dark oval: anyone with normal eyesight can find it quite easily. It is the great walled plain, one of the finest on the Moon, known as the Mare Crisium – the Sea of Crises. Three hundred miles in diameter – and almost completely surrounded by a ring of magnificent mountains, it had never been explored until we entered it in the late summer of 1996.

Our expedition was a large one. We had two heavy freighters which had flown our supplies and equipment from the main lunar base in the Mare Serenitatis, five hundred miles away. There were also three small rockets which were intended for short-range transport over regions which our surface vehicles could not cross. Luckily, most of the Mare Crisium is very flat. There are none of the great crevasses so common and so dangerous elsewhere, and very few craters or mountains of any size. As far as we could tell, our powerful caterpillar tractors would have no difficulty in taking us wherever we wished.

I was geologist – or selenologist, if you want to be pedantic – in charge of the group exploring the southern region of the Mare. We had crossed a hundred miles of it in a week, skirting the foothills of the mountains along the shore of what was once the ancient sea, some thousand million years before. When life was beginning on Earth, it was already dying here. The waters were retreating down the flanks of those stupendous cliffs, retreating into the empty heart of the Moon. Over the land which we were crossing, the tideless ocean had once been half a mile deep and now the only trace of moisture was the hoar frost one could sometimes find in caves which the searing sunlight never penetrated.

We had begun our journey early in the slow lunar dawn, and still had almost a week of Earth-time before nightfall. Half a dozen times a day we would leave our vehicle and go outside in the space-suits to hunt for interesting minerals, or to place markers for the guidance of future travellers. It was an uneventful routine. There is nothing hazardous or even particularly exciting about lunar exploration. We could live comfortably for a month in our pressurized tractors, and if we ran into trouble we could always radio for help and sit tight until one of the spaceships came to our rescue. When that happened there was always a frightful outcry about the waste of rocket fuel, so a tractor sent out an SOS only in a real emergency.

I said just now that there was nothing exciting about lunar exploration, but of course that is not true. One could never grow tired of those incredible mountains, so much more rugged than the gentle hills of Earth. We never knew, as we rounded the capes and promontories of that vanished sea, what new splendours would be revealed to us. The whole southern curve of the Mare Crisium is a vast delta where a score of rivers had once found their way into the ocean, fed perhaps by the torrential rains that must have lashed the mountains in the brief volcanic age when the moon was young. Each of these ancient valleys was an invitation, challenging us to climb into the unknown uplands beyond. But we had a hundred miles still to cover, and could only look longingly at the heights which others must scale.

We kept Earth-time aboard the tractor, and precisely at 22.00 hours the final radio message would be sent out to

114

base and we could close down for the day. Outside, the rocks would still be burning beneath the almost vertical sun, but to us it was night until we awoke again eight hours later. Then one of us would prepare breakfast, there would be a great buzzing of electric shavers and someone would switch on the short-wave radio from Earth. Indeed, when the smell of frying bacon began to fill the cabin, it was sometimes hard to believe that we were not back on our own world – everything was so normal and homely, apart from the feeling of decreased weight and the unnatural slowness with which objects fell.

It was my turn to prepare breakfast in the corner of the main cabin that served as a galley. I can remember that moment quite vividly after all these years, for the radio had just played one of my favourite melodies, the old Welsh air, 'David of the White Rock'. Our driver was already outside in his space-suit, inspecting our caterpillar treads. My assistant, Louis Garnett, was up forward in the control position, making some belated entries in yesterday's log.

As I stood by the frying-pan, waiting, like any terrestrial housewife, for the sausages to brown, I let my gaze wander idly over the mountain walls which covered the whole of the southern horizon, marching out of sight to the east and west below the curve of the Moon. They seemed only a mile or two from the tractor, but I knew that the nearest was twenty miles away. On the Moon, of course, there is no loss of detail with distance – none of that almost imperceptible haziness which softens and sometimes transfigures all far-off things on Earth.

Those mountains were ten thousand feet high, and they climbed steeply out of the plain as if ages ago some subterranean eruption had smashed them skywards through the molten crust. The base of even the nearest was hidden from sight by the steeply curving surface of the plain, for the Moon is a very little world, and from where I was standing

115

the horizon was only two miles away.

I lifted my eyes towards the peaks which no man had ever climbed, the peaks which, before the coming of terrestrial life, had watched the retreating oceans sink sullenly into their graves, taking with them the hope and morning promise of a world. The sunlight was beating against those ramparts with a glare that hurt the eyes, yet only a little way above them the stars were shining steadily in a sky blacker than a winter midnight on Earth.

I was turning away when my eye caught a metallic glitter high on the ridge of a great promontory thrusting out into the sea thirty miles to the west. It was a dimensionless point of light as if a star had been clawed from the sky by one of those cruel peaks, and I imagined that some smooth rock-surface was catching the sunlight and heliographing it straight into my eyes. Such things were not uncommon. When the Moon is in her second quarter, observers on Earth can sometimes see the great ranges in the Oceanus Procellarum burning with a blue-white iridescence as the sunlight flashes from their slopes and leaps again from world to world. But I was curious to know what kind of rock could be shining so brightly up there, and I climbed into the observation turret and swung our four-inch telescope round to the west.

I could see just enough to tantalize me. Clear and sharp in the field of vision, the mountain peaks seemed only half a mile away, but whatever was catching the sunlight was still too small to be resolved. Yet it seemed to have an elusive symmetry, and the summit upon which it rested was curiously flat. I stared for a long time at that glittering enigma, straining my eyes into space, until presently a smell of burning from the galley told me that our breakfast sausages had made their quarter-million-mile journey in vain.

All that morning we argued our way across the Mare

Crisium while the western mountains reared higher in the sky. Even when we were out prospecting in the space-suits, the discussion would continue over the radio. It was absolutely certain, my companions argued, that there had never been any form of intelligent life on the Moon. The only living things that had ever existed there were a few primitive plants and their slightly less degenerate ancestors. I knew that as well as anyone, but there are times when a scientist must not be afraid to make a fool of himself.

'Listen,' I said at last, 'I'm going up there, if only for my own peace of mind. That mountain's less than twelve thousand feet high – that's only two thousand under Earth gravity – and I can make the trip in twenty hours at the outside. I've always wanted to go up into those hills, anyway, and this gives me an excellent excuse.'

'If you don't break your neck,' said Garnett, 'you'll be the laughing-stock of the expedition when we get back to Base. That mountain will probably be called Wilson's Folly from now on.'

'I won't break my neck,' I said firmly. 'Who was the first man to climb Pico and Helicon?'

'But weren't you rather younger in those days?' asked Louis gently.

'That,' I said with great dignity, 'is as good a reason as any for going.'

We went to bed early that night, after driving the tractor to within half a mile of the promontory. Garnett was coming with me in the morning; he was a good climber, and had often been with me on such exploits before. Our driver was only too glad to be left in charge of the machine.

At first sight, those cliffs seemed completely unscalable, but to anyone with a good head for heights, climbing is easy on a world where all weights are only a sixth of their normal value. The real danger in lunar mountaineering lies in overconfidence; a six-hundred-foot drop on the Moon can kill

117

you just as thoroughly as a hundred-foot fall on Earth.

We made our first halt on a wide ledge about four thousand feet above the plain. Climbing had not been very difficult but my limbs were stiff with the unaccustomed effort, and I was glad of the rest. We could still see the tractor as a tiny metal insect far down at the foot of the cliff, and we reported our progress to the driver before starting on the next ascent.

Hour by hour the horizon widened and more and more of the great plain came into sight. Now we could look for fifty miles out across the Mare, and even see the peaks of the mountains on the opposite coast more than a hundred miles away. Few of the great lunar plains are as smooth as the Mare Crisium, and we could almost imagine that a sea of water and not of rock was lying there two miles below. Only a group of crater pits low down on the skyline spoiled the illusion.

Our goal was still invisible over the crest of the mountain and we were steering by maps, using the Earth as a guide. Almost due east of us, that great silver crescent hung low over the plain, already well into its first quarter. The Sun and the stars would make their slow march across the sky and would sink presently from sight, but Earth would always be there, never moving from her appointed place, waxing and waning as the years and seasons passed. In ten days' time she would be a blinding disc bathing these rocks with her midnight radiance, fifty-fold brighter than the full moon. But we must be out of the mountains long before night, or else we would remain among them forever.

Inside our suits it was comfortably cool, for the refrigeration units were fighting the fierce Sun and carrying away the body-heat of our exertions. We seldom spoke to each other, except to pass climbing instructions and to discuss our best plan of ascent. I do not know what Garnett was thinking, probably that this was the craziest goose chase he had ever embarked upon. I more than half agreed with him, but the joy of climbing, the knowledge that no man had ever gone this way before and the exhilaration of the steadily widening landscape gave me all the reward I needed.

I do not think I was particularly excited when I saw in front of us the wall of rock I had first inspected through the telescope from thirty miles away. It would level off about fifty feet above our heads, and there on the plateau would be the thing that had lured me over these barren wastes. It was, almost certainly, nothing more than a boulder splintered ages ago by a falling meteor, and with its cleavage planes still fresh and bright in this incorruptible, unchanging silence.

There were no hand-holds on the rock face and we had to use a grapnel. My tired arms seemed to gain new strength as I swung the three-pronged metal anchor round my head and sent it sailing up towards the stars. The first time it broke loose and came falling slowly back when we pulled the rope. On the third attempt, the prongs gripped firmly and our combined weights could not shift it.

Garnett looked at me anxiously. I could tell that he wanted to go first, but I smiled back at him through the glass of my helmet and shook my head. Slowly, taking my time, I began the final ascent.

Even with my space-suit, I only weighed forty pounds here, so I pulled myself up hand over hand without bothering to use my feet. At the rim I paused and waved to my companion, then I scrambled over the edge and stood upright, staring ahead of me.

You must understand that until this very moment I had been almost completely convinced that there could be nothing strange or unusual for me to find here. Almost, but not quite; it was that haunting doubt that had driven me forwards. Well, it was a doubt no longer, but the haunting had scarcely begun.

I was standing on a plateau perhaps a hundred feet across. It had once been smooth – too smooth to be natural – but falling meteors had pitted and scored its surface through immeasurable aeons. It had been levelled to support a glittering roughly pyramidal structure, twice as high as a man, that was set in the rock like a gigantic, many-faceted jewel.

Probably no emotion at all filled my mind in those first few seconds. Then I felt a great lifting of my heart, and a strange inexpressible joy. For I loved the Moon, and now I knew that the creeping moss of Aristarchus and Eratosthenes was not the only life she had brought forth in her youth. The old, discredited dream of the first explorers was true. There had, after all, been a lunar civilization – and I was the first to find it. That I had come perhaps a hundred million years too late did not distress me; it was enough to have come at all.

My mind was beginning to function normally, to analyse and to ask questions. Was this a building, a shrine – or something for which my language had no name? If a building, then why was it erected in so uniquely inaccessible a spot? I wondered if it might be a temple, and I could picture the adepts of some strange priesthood calling on their gods to preserve them as the life of the Moon ebbed with the dying oceans, and calling on their gods in vain.

I took a dozen steps forward to examine the thing more closely, but some sense of caution kept me from going too near. I knew a little of archaeology, and tried to guess the cultural level of the civilization that must have smoothed this mountain and raised the glittering mirror surfaces that still dazzled my eyes.

The Egyptians could have done it, I thought, if their workmen had possessed whatever strange materials these far more ancient architects had used. Because of the thing's smallness, it did not occur to me that I might be looking at the handiwork of a race more advanced than my own. The idea that the Moon had possessed intelligence at all was still almost too tremendous to grasp, and my pride would not let me take the final, humiliating plunge.

And then I noticed something that set the scalp crawling at the back of my neck – something so trivial and so innocent that many would never have noticed it at all. I have said that the plateau was scarred by meteors; it was also coated inches deep with the cosmic dust that is always filtering down upon the surface of any world where there are no winds to disturb it. Yet the dust and the meteor scratches ended quite abruptly in a wide circle enclosing the little pyramid, as though an invisible wall was protecting it from the ravages of time and the slow but ceaseless bombardment from space.

There was someone shouting in my earphones, and I realized that Garnett had been calling me for some time. I walked unsteadily to the edge of the cliff and signalled him to join me, not trusting myself to speak. Then I went back towards that circle in the dust. I picked up a fragment of splintered rock and tossed it gently towards the shining enigma. If the pebble had vanished at that invisible barrier I should not have been surprised, but it seemed to hit a smooth, hemispherical surface and slide gently to the ground.

I knew then that I was looking at nothing that could be matched in the antiquity of my own race. This was not a building, but a machine, protecting itself with forces that had challenged Eternity. Those forces, whatever they might be, were still operating, and perhaps I had already come too close. I thought of all the radiations man had trapped and tamed in the past century. For all I knew, I might be as irrevocably doomed as if I had stepped into the deadly, silent aura of an unshielded atomic pile.

I remember turning then towards Garnett, who had

joined me and was now standing motionless at my side. He seemed quite oblivious of me, so I did not disturb him but walked to the edge of the cliff in an effort to marshal my thoughts. There below me lay the Mare Crisium – Sea of Crises, indeed – strange and weird to most men, but reassuringly familiar to me. I lifted my eyes towards the crescent Earth, lying in her cradle of stars, and I wondered what her clouds had covered when these unknown builders had finished their work. Was it the steaming jungle of the Carboniferous, the bleak shoreline over which the first amphibians must crawl to conquer the land – or, earlier still, the long loneliness before the coming of life?

Do not ask me why I did not guess the truth sooner – the truth that seems so obvious now. In the first excitement of my discovery, I had assumed without question that this crystalline apparition had been built by some race belonging to the Moon's remote past, but suddenly, and with overwhelming force, the belief came to me that it was as alien to the Moon as I myself.

In twenty years we had found no trace of life but a few degenerate plants. No lunar civilization, whatever its doom, could have left but a single token of its existence.

I looked at the shining pyramid again, and the more remote it seemed from anything that had to do with the Moon. And suddenly I felt myself shaking with a foolish, hysterical laughter, brought on by excitement and over-exertion: for I had imagined that the little pyramid was speaking to me and was saying: 'Sorry, I'm a stranger here myself.'

It has taken us twenty years to crack that invisible shield and to reach the machine inside those crystal walls. What we could not understand, we broke at last with the savage might of atomic power and now I have seen the fragments of the lovely, glittering thing I found up there on the mountain.

They are meaningless. The mechanisms – if indeed they are mechanisms – of the pyramid belong to a technology that lies far beyond our horizon, perhaps to the technology of paraphysical forces.

The mystery haunts us all the more now that the other planets have been reached and we know that only Earth has ever been the home of intelligent life. Nor could any lost civilization of our own world have built that machine, for the thickness of the meteoric dust on the plateau has enabled us to measure its age. It was set there upon its mountain before life had emerged from the seas of Earth.

When our world was half its present age, *something* from the stars swept through the Solar System, left this token of its passage, and went again upon its way. Until we destroyed it, that machine was still fulfilling the purpose of its builders; and as to that purpose, here is my guess.

Nearly a hundred thousand million stars are turning in the circle of the Milky Way, and long ago other races on the worlds of other suns must have scaled and passed the heights that we have reached. Think of such civilizations, far back in time against the fading afterglow of Creation, masters of a universe so young that life as yet had come only to a handful of worlds. Theirs would have been a loneliness we cannot imagine, the loneliness of gods looking out across infinity and finding none to share their thoughts.

They must have searched the star-clusters as we have searched the planets. Everywhere there would be worlds, but they would be empty or peopled with crawling, mindless things. Such was our own Earth, the smoke of the great volcanoes still staining the skies, when that first ship of the peoples of the dawn came sliding in from the abyss beyond Pluto. It passed the frozen outer worlds, knowing that life could play no part in their destinies. It came to rest among the inner planets, warming themselves around the fire of the Sun and waiting for their stories to begin.

Those wanderers must have looked on Earth, circling safely in the narrow zone between fire and ice, and must have guessed that it was the favourite of the Sun's children. Here, in the distant future, would be intelligence; but there were countless stars before them still, and they might never come this way again.

So they left a sentinel, one of millions they have scattered throughout the universe, watching over all worlds with the promise of life. It was a beacon that down the ages has been patiently signalling the fact that no one had discovered it.

Perhaps you understand now why that crystal pyramid was set upon the Moon instead of on the Earth. Its builders were not concerned with races still struggling up from savagery. They would be interested in our civilization only if we proved our fitness to survive – by crossing space and so escaping from the Earth, our cradle. That is the challenge that all intelligent races must meet, sooner or later. It is a double challenge, for it depends in turn upon the conquest of atomic energy and the last choice between life and death.

Once we had passed that crisis, it was only a matter of time before we found the pyramid and forced it open. Now its signals have ceased, and those whose duty it is will be turning their minds upon Earth. Perhaps they wish to help our infant civilization. But they must be very, very old, and the old are often insanely jealous of the young.

I can never look now at the Milky Way without wondering from which of those banked clouds of stars the emissaries are coming. If you will pardon so commonplace a simile, we have broken the glass of the fire-alarm and have nothing to do but to wait.

I do not think we will have to wait for long.

THE STAR

It is three thousand light-years to the Vatican. Once, I believed that space could have no power over faith, just as I believed that the heavens declared the glory of God's handiwork. Now I have seen that handiwork, and my faith is sorely troubled. I stare at the crucifix that hangs on the cabin wall above the Mark VI Computer, and for the first time in my life I wonder if it is no more than an empty symbol.

I have told no one yet, but the truth cannot be concealed. The facts are there for all to read, recorded on the count less miles of magnetic tape and the thousands of photographs we are carrying back to Earth. Other scientists can interpret them as easily as I can, and I am not one who would condone that tampering with the truth which often gave my order a bad name in the olden days.

The crew are already sufficiently depressed: I wonder how they will take this ultimate irony. Few of them have any religious faith, yet they will not relish using this final weapon in their campaign against me – that private, good-natured, but fundamentally serious, war which lasted all the way from Earth. It amused them to have a Jesuit as chief astrophysicist: Dr. Chandler, for instance, could never get over it (why are medical men such notorious atheists?). Sometimes he would meet me on the observation deck, where the lights are always low so that the stars shine with undiminished glory. He would come up to me in the gloom and stand staring out of the great oval port, while the heavens crawled slowly around us as the ship turned end over end with the residual spin we had never bothered to correct.

'Well, Father,' he would say at last, 'it goes on forever and forever, and perhaps *Something* made it. But how you can believe that Something has a special interest in us and our miserable little world – that just beats me.' Then the argument would start, while the stars and nebulae would swing around us in silent, endless arcs beyond the flawlessly clear plastic of the observation port.

It was, I think, the apparent incongruity of my position that caused most amusement to the crew. In vain I would point to my three papers in the *Astrophysical Journal*, my five in the *Monthly Notices of the Royal Astronomical Society*. I would remind them that my order has long been famous for its scientific works. We may be few now, but ever since the eighteenth century we have made contributions to astronomy and geophysics out of all proportion to our numbers. Will my report on the Phoenix Nebula end our thousand years of history? It will end, I fear, much more than that.

I do not know who gave the nebula its name, which seems to me a very bad one. If it contains a prophecy, it is one that cannot be verified for several billion years. Even the word nebula is misleading: this is a far smaller object than those stupendous clouds of mist – the stuff of unborn stars – that are scattered throughout the length of the Milky Way. On the cosmic scale, indeed, the Phoenix Nebula is a tiny thing – a tenuous shell of gas surrounding a single star.

Or what is left of a star ...

The Rubens engraving of Loyola seems to mock me as it hangs there above the spectrophotometer tracings. What would *you*, Father, have made of this knowledge that has come into my keeping, so far from the little world that was all the universe you knew? Would your faith have risen to the challenge, as mine has failed to do?

You gaze into the distance, Father, but I have travelled

a distance beyond any that you could have imagined when you founded our order a thousand years ago. No other survey ship has been so far from Earth: we are at the very frontiers of the explored universe. We set out to reach the Phoenix Nebula, we succeeded, and we are homeward bound with our burden of knowledge. I wish I could lift that burden from my shoulders, but I call to you in vain across the centuries and the light-years that lie between us.

On the book you are holding the words are plain to read. AD MAIOREM DEI GLORIAM, the message runs, but it is a message I can no longer believe. Would you still believe it, if you could see what we have found?

We knew, of course, what the Phoenix Nebula was. Every year, in our galaxy alone, more than a hundred stars explode, blazing for a few hours or days with thousands of times their normal brilliance before they sink back into death and obscurity. Such are the ordinary novae – the commonplace disasters of the universe. I have recorded the spectrograms and light curves of dozens since I started working at the Lunar Observatory.

But three or four times in every thousand years occurs something beside which even a nova pales into total insignificance.

When a star becomes a *supernova*, it may for a little while outshine all the massed suns of the galaxy. The Chinese astronomers watched this happen in A.D. 1054, not knowing what it was they saw. Five centuries later, in 1572, a supernova blazed in Cassiopeia so brilliantly that it was visible in the daylight sky. There have been three more in the thousand years that have passed since then.

Our mission was to visit the remnants of such a catastrophe, to reconstruct the events that led up to it, and, if possible, to learn its cause. We came slowly in through the concentric shells of gas that had been blasted out six thousand years before, yet were expanding still. They were

127

immensely hot, radiating even now with a fierce violet light, but were far too tenuous to do us any damage. When the star had exploded, its outer layers had been driven upwards with such speed that they had escaped completely from its gravitational field. Now they formed a hollow shell large enough to engulf a thousand solar systems, and at its centre burned the tiny, fantastic object which the star had now become – a white dwarf, smaller than the Earth, yet weighing a million times as much.

The glowing gas shells were all around us, banishing the normal night of interstellar space. We were flying into the centre of a cosmic bomb that had detonated millennia ago and whose incandescent fragments were still hurtling apart. The immense scale of the explosion, and the fact that the debris already covered a volume of space many billions of miles across, robbed the scene of any visible movement. It would take decades before the unaided eye could detect any motion in these tortured wisps and eddies of gas, yet the sense of turbulent expansion was overwhelming.

We had checked our primary drive hours before, and were drifting slowly towards the fierce little star ahead. Once it had been a sun like our own, but it had squandered in a few hours the energy that should have kept it shining for a million years. Now it was a shrunken miser, hoarding its resources as if trying to make amends for its prodigal youth.

No one seriously expected to find planets. If there had been any before the explosion, they would have been boiled into puffs of vapour, and their substance lost in the greater wreckage of the star itself. But we made the automatic search, as we always do when approaching an unknown sun, and presently we found a single small world circling the star at an immense distance. It must have been the Pluto of this vanished solar system, orbiting on the frontiers of the night. Too far from the central sun ever to have known life, its remoteness had saved it from the fate of all its lost companions.

The passing fires had seared its rocks and burned away the mantle of frozen gas that must have covered it in the days before the disaster. We landed, and we found the Vault.

Its builders had made sure that we should. The monolithic marker that stood above the entrance was now a fused stump, but even the first long-range photographs told us that here was the work of intelligence. A little later we detected the continent-wide pattern of radioactivity that had been buried in the rock. Even if the pylon above the Vault had been destroyed, this would have remained, an immovable and all but eternal beacon calling to the stars. Our ship fell towards this gigantic bull's-eye like an arrow into its target.

The pylon must have been a mile high when it was built, but now it looked like a candle that had melted down into a puddle of wax. It took us a week to drill through the fused rock, since we did not have the proper tools for a task like this. We were astronomers, not archaeologists, but we could improvise. Our original purpose was forgotten: this lonely monument, reared with such labour at the greatest possible distance from the doomed sun, could have only one meaning. A civilization that knew it was about to die had made its last bid for immortality.

It will take us generations to examine all the treasures that were placed in the Vault. They had plenty of time to prepare, for their sun must have given its first warnings many years before the final detonation. Everything that they wished to preserve, all the fruit of their genius, they brought here to this distant world in the days before the end, hoping that some other race would find it and that they would not be utterly forgotten. Would we have done as well, or would we have been too lost in our own misery to give thought to a future we could never see or share?

If only they had had a little more time! They could travel freely enough between the planets of their own sun, but they had not yet learned to cross the interstellar gulfs, and the nearest solar system was a hundred light-years away. Yet even had they possessed the secret of the Transfinite Drive no more than a few millions could have been saved. Perhaps it was better thus.

Even if they had not been so disturbingly human as their sculpture shows, we could not have helped admiring them and grieving for their fate. They left thousands of visual records and the machines for projecting them, together with elaborate pictorial instructions from which it will not be difficult to learn their written language. We have examined many of these records, and brought to life for the first time in six thousand years the warmth and beauty of a civilization that in many ways must have been superior to our own. Perhaps they only showed us the best, and one can hardly blame them. But their worlds were very lovely, and their cities were built with a grace that matches anything of man's. We have watched them at work and play, and listened to their musical speech sounding across the centuries. One scene is still before my eyes – a group of children on a beach of strange blue sand, playing in the waves as children play on Earth. Curious whiplike trees line the shore, and some very large animal is wading in the shallows yet attracting no attention at all.

And sinking into the sea, still warm and friendly and life-giving, is the sun that will turn traitor and obliterate all this innocent happiness.

Perhaps if we had not been so far from home and so vulnerable to loneliness, we should not have been so deeply moved. Many of us had seen the ruins of ancient civilizations on other worlds, but they had never affected us so profoundly. This tragedy was unique. It is one thing for a race to fail and die, as nations and cultures have done on

130

Earth. But to be destroyed so completely in the full flower of its achievement, leaving no survivors – now could that be reconciled with the mercy of God?

My colleagues have asked me that, and I have given what answers I can. Perhaps you could have done better, Father Loyola, but I have found nothing in the *Exercitia Spiritualia* that helps me here. They were not an evil people: I do not know what gods they worshipped, if indeed they worshipped any. But I have looked back at them across the centuries, and have watched while the loveliness they used their last strength to preserve was brought forth again into the light of their shrunken sun. They could have taught us much: why were they destroyed?

I know the answers that my colleagues will give when they get back to Earth. They will say that the universe has no purpose and no plan, that since a hundred suns explode every year in our galaxy, at this very moment some race is dying in the depths of space. Whether that race has done good or evil during its lifetime will make no difference in the end: there is no divine justice, for there is no God.

Yet, of course, what we have seen proves nothing of the sort. Anyone who argues thus is being swayed by emotion, not logic. God has no need to justify His actions to man. He who built the universe can destroy it when He chooses. It is arrogance – it is perilously near blasphemy – for us to say what He may or may not do.

This I could have accepted, hard though it is to look upon whole worlds and peoples thrown into the furnace. But there comes a point when even the deepest faith must falter, and now, as I look at the calculations lying before me, I know I have reached that point at last.

We could not tell, before we reached the nebula, how long ago the explosion took place. Now, from the astronomical evidence and the record in the rocks of that one surviving planet, I have been able to date it very exactly. I know in what year the light of this colossal conflagration reached our Earth. I know how brilliantly the supernova whose corpse now dwindles behind our speeding ship once shone in terrestrial skies. I know how it must have blazed low in the east before sunrise, like a beacon in that oriental dawn.

There can be no reasonable doubt: the ancient mystery is solved at last. Yet, oh God, there were so many stars you could have used. What was the need to give these people to the fire, that the symbol of their passing might shine above Bethlehem?

REFUGEE

'WHEN he comes aboard,' said Captain Saunders, as he waited for the landing ramp to extrude itself, 'what the devil shall I call him?'

There was a thoughtful silence while the navigation officer and the assistant pilot considered this problem in etiquette. Then Mitchell locked the main control panel, and the ship's multitudinous mechanisms lapsed into unconsciousness as power was withdrawn from them.

'The correct address,' he drawled slowly, 'is "Your Royal Highness".'

'Huh!' snorted the captain. 'I'll be damned if I'll call anyone that!'

'In these progressive days,' put in Chambers helpfully, 'I believe that "Sir" is quite sufficient. But there's no need to worry if you forget: it's been a long time since anyone went to the Tower. Besides, this Henry isn't as tough a proposition as the one who had all the wives.'

'From all accounts,' added Mitchell, 'he's a very pleasant young man. Quite intelligent, too. He's often been known to ask people technical questions that they couldn't answer.'

Captain Saunders ignored the implications of this remark, beyond resolving that if Prince Henry wanted to know how a Field Compensation Drive Generator worked, then Mitchell could do the explaining. He got gingerly to his feet – they'd been operating on half a gravity during flight, and now they were on Earth, he felt like a ton of bricks – and started to make his way along the corridors that led to the lower air lock. With an oily purring, the great curving door side-stepped out of his way. Adjusting his smile, he walked out to meet the television cameras and the heir to the British throne.

The man who would, presumably, one day be Henry IX of England was still in his early twenties. He was slightly below average height, and had fine-drawn, regular features that really lived up to all the genealogical clichés. Captain Saunders, who came from Dallas and had no intention of being impressed by any prince, found himself unexpectedly moved by the wide, sad eyes. They were eyes that had seen too many receptions and parades, that had had to watch countless totally uninteresting things, that had never been allowed to stray far from the carefully planned official routes. Looking at that proud but weary face, Captain Saunders glimpsed for the first time the ultimate loneliness of royalty. All his dislike of that institution became suddenly trivial against its real defect: what was wrong with the Crown was the unfairness of inflicting such a burden on any human being ...

The passageways of the *Centaurus* were too narrow to allow for general sight-seeing, and it was soon clear that it suited Prince Henry very well to leave his entourage behind. Once they had begun moving through the ship, Saunders lost all his stiffness and reserve, and within a few minutes was treating the prince exactly like any other visitor. He did not realize that one of the earliest lessons royalty has to learn is that of putting people at their ease.

'You know, Captain,' said the prince wistfully, 'this is a big day for us. I've always hoped that one day it would be possible for spaceships to operate from England. But it still seems strange to have a port of our own here, after all these years. Tell me – did you ever have much to do with rockets?'

'Well, I had some training on them, but they were already on the way out before I graduated. I was lucky: some older men had to go back to school and start all over again – or

134

else abandon space completely if they couldn't convert to the new ships.'

'It made as much difference as that?'

'Oh yes – when the rocket went, it was as big as the change from sail to steam. That's an analogy you'll often hear, by the way. There was a glamour about the old rockets, just as there was about the old windjammers, which these modern ships haven't got. When the *Centaurus* takes off, she goes up as quietly as a balloon – and as slowly, if she wants to. But a rocket blast-off shook the ground for miles, and you'd be deaf for days if you were too near the launching apron. Still, you'll know all that from the old news recordings.'

The prince smiled.

'Yes,' he said. 'I've often run through them at the Palace. I think I've watched every incident in all the pioneering expeditions. I was sorry to see the end of the rockets, too. But we could never have had a spaceport here on Salisbury Plain – the vibration would have shaken down Stonehenge!'

'Stonehenge?' queried Saunders as he held open a hatch and let the prince through into Hold Number 3.

'Ancient monument – one of the most famous stone circles in the world. It's really impressive, and about three thousand years old. See it if you can – it's only ten miles from here.'

Captain Saunders had some difficulty in suppressing a smile. What an odd country this was: where else, he wondered, would you find contrasts like this? It made him feel very young and raw when he remembered that back home Billy the Kid was ancient history, and there was hardly anything in the whole of Texas as much as five hundred years old. For the first time he began to realize what tradition meant: it gave Prince Henry something that he could never possess. Poise – self-confidence, yes, that was it. And a pride that was somehow free from arrogance because it took itself so much for granted that it never had to be asserted.

It was surprising how many questions Prince Henry managed to ask in the thirty minutes that had been allotted for his tour of the freighter. They were not the routine questions that people asked out of politeness, quite uninterested in the answers. H.R.H. Prince Henry knew a lot about spaceships, and Captain Saunders felt completely exhausted when he handed his distinguished guest back to the reception committee, which had been waiting outside the *Centaurus* with well-simulated patience.

'Thank you very much, Captain,' said the prince as they shook hands in the air lock. 'I've not enjoyed myself so much for ages. I hope you have a pleasant stay in England, and a successful voyage.' Then his retinue whisked him away, and the port officials frustrated until now, came aboard to check the ship's papers.

'Well,' said Mitchell when it was all over, 'what did you think of our Prince of Wales?'

'He surprised me,' answered Saunders frankly. 'I'd never have guessed he was a prince. I always thought they were rather dumb. But heck, he *knew* the principles of the Field Drive! Has he ever been up in space?'

'Once, I think. Just a hop above the atmosphere in a Space Force ship. It didn't even reach orbit before it came back again – but the Prime Minister nearly had a fit. There were questions in the House and editorials in *The Times*. Everyone decided that the heir to the throne was too valuable to risk in these newfangled inventions. So though he has the rank of commodore in the Royal Space Force, he's never even been to the moon.'

'The poor guy,' said Captain Saunders.

He had three days to burn, since it was not the captain's

136

job to supervise the loading of the ship or the preflight maintenance. Saunders knew skippers who hung around breathing heavily on the necks of the servicing engineers, but he wasn't that type. Besides, he wanted to see London. He had been to Mars and Venus and the moon, but this was his first visit to England. Mitchell and Chambers filled him with useful information and put him on the monorail to London before dashing off to see their own families. They would be returning to the spaceport a day before he did, to see that everything was in order. It was a great relief having officers one could rely on so implicitly; they were unimaginative and cautious, but thorough going almost to a fault. If *they* said that everything was ship-shape, Saunders knew he could take off without qualms.

The sleek, streamlined cylinder whistled across the carefully tailored landscape. It was so close to the ground, and travelling so swiftly, that one could only gather fleeting impressions of the towns and fields that flashed by. Everything, thought Saunders, was so incredibly compact, and on such a Lilliputian scale. There were no open spaces, no fields more than a mile long in any direction. It was enough to give a Texan claustrophobia – particularly a Texan who also happened to be a space pilot.

The sharply defined edge of London appeared like the bulwark of some walled city on the horizon. With few exceptions, the buildings were quite low – perhaps fifteen or twenty storeys in height. The monorail shot through a narrow canyon, over a very attractive park, across a river that was presumably the Thames, and then came to rest with a steady, powerful surge of deceleration. A loudspeaker announced, in a modest voice that seemed afraid of being overheard: 'This is Paddington. Passengers for the North please remain seated.' Saunders pulled his baggage down from the rack and headed out into the station.

As he made for the entrance to the Underground, he

passed a bookstall and glanced at the magazines on display. About half of them, it seemed, carried photographs of Prince Henry or other members of the royal family. This, thought Saunders, was altogether too much of a good thing. He also noticed that all the evening papers showed the prince entering or leaving the *Centaurus*, and bought copies to read in the subway – he begged its pardon, the 'Tube'.

The editorial comments had a monotonous similarity. At last, they rejoiced, England need no longer take a back seat among the space-going nations. Now it was possible to operate a space fleet without having a million square miles of desert: the silent, gravity-defying ships of today could land, if need be, in Hyde Park, without even disturbing the ducks on the Serpentine. Saunders found it odd that this sort of patriotism had managed to survive into the age of space, but he guessed that the British had felt it pretty badly when they'd had to borrow launching sites from the Australians, the Americans and the Russians.

The London Underground was still, after a century and a half, the best transport system in the world, and it deposited Saunders safely at his destination less than ten minutes after he had left Paddington. In ten minutes the *Centaurus* could have covered fifty thousand miles; but space, after all, was not quite so crowded as this. Nor were the orbits of space craft so tortuous as the streets Saunders had to negotiate to reach his hotel. All attempts to straighten out London had failed dismally, and it was fifteen minutes before he completed the last hundred yards of his journey.

He stripped off his jacket and collapsed thankfully on his bed. Three quiet, carefree days all to himself: it seemed too good to be true.

It was. He had barely taken a deep breath when the phone rang.

'Captain Saunders? I'm so glad we found you. This is

138

the B.B.C. We have a programme called "In Town Tonight" and we were wondering ...'

The thud of the air-lock door was the sweetest sound Saunders had heard for days. Now he was safe: nobody could get at him here in his armoured fortress, which would soon be far out in the freedom of space. It was not that he had been treated badly: on the contrary, he had been treated altogether too well. He had made four (or was it five?) appearances on various TV programmes; he had been to more parties than he could remember; he had acquired several hundred new friends and (the way his head felt now) forgotten all his old ones.

'Who started the rumour,' he said to Mitchell as they met at the port, 'that the British were reserved and stand-offish? Heaven help me if I ever meet a *demonstrative* Englishman.'

'I take it,' replied Mitchell, 'that you had a good time.'

'Ask me tomorrow,' Saunders replied. 'I may have re-integrated my psyche by then.'

'I saw you on that quiz programme last night,' remarked Chambers. 'You looked pretty ghastly.'

'Thank you: that's just the sort of sympathetic encouragement I need at the moment. I'd like to see you think of a synonym for "jejune" after you'd been up until three in the morning.'

'Vapid,' replied Chambers promptly.

'Insipid,' said Mitchell, not to be outdone.

'You win. Let's have those overhaul schedules and see what the engineers have been up to.'

Once seated at the control desk, Captain Saunders quickly became his usual efficient self. He was home again, and his training took over. He knew exactly what to do, and would do it with automatic precision. To right and left of him, Mitchell and Chambers were checking their instruments and calling the control tower.

It took them an hour to carry out the elaborate pre-flight routine. When the last signature had been attached to the last sheet of instructions, and the last red light on the monitor panel had turned to green, Saunders flopped back in his seat and lit a cigarette. They had ten minutes to spare before take-off.

'One day,' he said, 'I'm going to come to England incognito to find what makes the place tick. I don't understand how you can crowd so many people on to one little island without it sinking.'

'Huh,' snorted Chambers. 'You should see Holland. That makes England look as wide open as Texas.'

'And then there's this royal family business. Do you know, wherever I went everybody kept asking me how I got on with Prince Henry – what we'd talked about – didn't I think he was a fine guy, and so on. Frankly, I got fed up with it. I can't imagine how you've managed to stand it for a thousand years.'

'Don't think that the royal family's been popular all the time,' replied Mitchell. 'Remember what happened to Charles the First? And some of the things we said about the early Georges were quite as rude as the remarks your people made later.'

'We just happen to like tradition,' said Chambers. 'We're not afraid to change when the time comes, but as far as the royal family is concerned – well, it's unique and we're rather fond of it. Just the way you feel about the Statue of Liberty.'

'Not a fair example. I don't think it's right to put human beings up on a pedestal and treat them as if they're – well, minor deities. Look at Prince Henry, for instance. Do you think he'll ever have a chance of doing the things he really wants to do? I saw him three times on TV when I was in London. The first time he was opening a new school somewhere; then he was giving a speech to the Worshipful Company of Fishmongers at the Guildhall (I swear I'm not making *that* up), and finally he was receiving an address of welcome from the mayor of Podunk, or whatever your equivalent is.' ('Wigan,' interjected Mitchell.) 'I think I'd rather be in jail than live that sort of life. Why can't you leave the poor guy alone?'

For once, neither Mitchell nor Chambers rose to the challenge. Indeed, they maintained a somewhat frigid silence. That's torn it, thought Saunders. I should have kept my big mouth shut; now I've hurt their feelings. I should have remembered that advice I read somewhere: 'The British have two religions – cricket and the royal family. Never attempt to criticize either.'

The awkward pause was broken by the radio and the voice of the spaceport controller.

'Control to *Centaurus*. Your flight lane clear. O.K. to lift.'

'Take-off programme starting – *now*!' replied Saunders, throwing the master switch. Then he leaned back, his eyes taking in the entire control panel, his hands clear of the board but ready for instant action.

He was tense but completely confident. Better brains than his – brains of metal and crystal and flashing electron streams – were in charge of the *Centaurus* now. If necessary, he could take command, but he had never yet lifted a ship manually and never expected to do so. If the automatics failed, he would cancel the take-off and sit here on Earth until the fault had been cleared up.

The main field went on, and weight ebbed from the *Centaurus*. There were protesting groans from the ship's hull and structure as the strains redistributed themselves. The curved arms of the landing cradle were carrying no load now; the slightest breath of wind would carry the freighter away into the sky.

Control called from the tower: 'Your weight now zero: check calibration.'

Saunders looked at his meters. The upthrust of the field would now exactly equal the weight of the ship, and the meter readings should agree with the totals on the loading schedules. In at least one instance this check had revealed the presence of a stowaway on board a spaceship – the gauges were as sensitive as that.

'One million, five hundred and sixty thousand, four hundred and twenty kilograms,' Saunders read off from the thrust indicators. 'Pretty good – it checks to within fifteen kilos. The first time I've been underweight, though. You could have taken on some more candy for that plump girl friend of yours in Port Lowell, Mitch.'

The assistant pilot gave a rather sickly grin. He had never quite lived down a blind date on Mars which had given him a completely unwarranted reputation for preferring statuesque blondes.

There was no sense of motion, but the *Centaurus* was now falling up into the summer sky as her weight was not only neutralized but reversed. To the watchers below, she would be a swiftly mounting star, a silver globule climbing through and beyond the clouds. Around her, the blue of the atmosphere was deepening into the eternal darkness of space. Like a bead moving along an invisible wire, the freighter was following the pattern of radio waves that would lead her from world to world.

This, thought Captain Saunders, was his twenty-sixth take-off from Earth. But the wonder would never die, nor would he ever outgrow the feeling of power it gave him to sit here at the control panel, the master of forces beyond even the dreams of mankind's ancient gods. No two departures were ever the same: some were into the dawn, some towards the sunset, some above a cloud-veiled Earth, some through clear and sparkling skies. Space itself might

142

be unchanging, but on Earth the same pattern never recurred, and no man ever looked twice at the same landscape or the same sky. Down there the Atlantic waves were marching eternally towards Europe, and high above them – but so far below the *Centaurus*! – the glittering bands of cloud were advancing before the same winds. England began to merge into the Continent, and the European coastline became foreshortened and misty as it sank hull down beyond the curve of the world. At the frontier of the west, a fugitive stain on the horizon was the first hint of America. With a single glance, Captain Saunders could span all the leagues across which Columbus had laboured half a thousand years ago.

With the silence of limitless power, the ship shook itself free from the last bonds of Earth. To an outside observer, the only sign of the energies it was expending would have been the dull red glow from the radiation fins around the vessel's equator, as the heat loss from the mass-converters was dissipated into space.

'14:03:45,' wrote Captain Saunders neatly in the log. 'Escape velocity attained. Course deviation negligible.'

There was little point in making the entry. The modest 25,000 miles an hour that had been the almost unattainable goal of the first astronauts had no practical significance now, since the *Centaurus* was still accelerating and would continue to gain speed for hours. But it had a profound psychological meaning. Until this moment, if power had failed, they would have fallen back to Earth. But now gravity could never recapture them: they had achieved the freedom of space, and could take their pick of the planets. In practice, of course, there would be several kinds of hell to pay if they did not pick Mars and deliver their cargo according to plan. But Captain Saunders, like all spacemen, was fundamentally a romantic. Even on a milk run like this he would sometimes dream of the ringed glory of Saturn or the sombre

Neptunian wastes, lit by the distant fires of the shrunken sun.

An hour after take-off, according to the hallowed ritual, Chambers left the course computer to its own devices and produced the three glasses that lived beneath the chart table. As he drank the traditional toast to Newton, Oberth and Einstein, Saunders wondered how this little ceremony had originated. Space crews had certainly been doing it for at least sixty years: perhaps it could be traced back to the legendary rocket engineer who made the remark, 'I've burned more alcohol in sixty seconds than you've ever sold across this lousy bar.'

Two hours later, the last course correction that the tracking stations on Earth could give them had been fed into the computer. From now on, until Mars came sweeping up ahead, they were on their own. It was a lonely thought, yet a curiously exhilarating one. Saunders savoured it in his mind. There were just the three of them here – and no one else within a million miles.

In the circumstances, the detonation of an atomic bomb could hardly have been more shattering than the modest knock on the cabin door ...

Captain Saunders had never been so startled in his life. With a yelp that had already left him before he had a chance to suppress it, he shot out of his seat and rose a full yard before the ship's residual gravity field dragged him back. Chambers and Mitchell, on the other hand, behaved with traditional British phlegm. They swivelled in their bucket seats, stared at the door, and then waited for their captain to take action.

It took Saunders several seconds to recover. Had he been confronted with what might be called a normal emergency, he would already have been halfway into a space-suit. But a diffident knock on the door of the control cabin, when

144

everybody else in the ship was sitting beside him, was not a fair test.

A stowaway was simply impossible. The danger had been so obvious, right from the beginning of commercial space flight, that the most stringent precautions had been taken against it. One of his officers, Saunders knew, would always have been on duty during loading; no one could possibly have crept in unobserved. Then there had been the detailed pre-flight inspection, carried out by both Mitchell and Chambers. Finally, there was the weight check at the moment before take-off; *that* was conclusive. No, a stowaway was totally . . .

The knock on the door sounded again. Captain Saunders clenched his fists and squared his jaw. In a few minutes, he thought, some romantic idiot was going to be very, very sorry.

'Open the door, Mr. Mitchell,' Saunders growled. In a single long stride, the assistant pilot crossed the cabin and jerked open the hatch.

For an age, it seemed, no one spoke. Then the stowaway, wavering slightly in the low gravity, came into the cabin. He was completely self-possessed, and looked very pleased with himself.

'Good afternoon, Captain Saunders,' he said, 'I must apologize for this sudden intrusion.'

Saunders swallowed hard. Then, as the pieces of the jigsaw fell into place, he looked first at Mitchell, then at Chambers. Both of his officers stared guilelessly back at him with expressions of ineffable innocence. 'So *that's* it,' he said bitterly. There was no need for any explanations: everything was perfectly clear. It was easy to picture the complicated negotiations, the midnight meetings, the falsification of records, the off-loading of non-essential cargoes that his trusted colleagues had been conducting behind his back. He was sure it was a most interesting story, but he didn't want to hear about it now. He was too busy wondering what the *Manual of Space Law* would have to say about a situation like this, though he was already gloomily certain that it would be of no use to him at all.

It was too late to turn back, of course: the conspirators wouldn't have made an elementary miscalculation like that. He would just have to make the best of what looked to be the trickiest voyage in his career.

He was still trying to think of something to say when the PRIORITY signal started flashing on the radio board. The stowaway looked at his watch.

'I was expecting that,' he said. 'It's probably the Prime Minister. I think I'd better speak to the poor man.'

Saunders thought so too.

'Very well, Your Royal Highness,' he said sulkily, and with such emphasis that the title sounded almost like an insult. Then, feeling much put upon, he retired into a corner.

It was the Prime Minister all right, and he sounded very upset. Several times he used the phrase 'your duty to your people' and once there was a distinct catch in his throat as he said something about 'devotion of your subjects to the Crown.' Saunders realized, with some surprise, that he really meant it.

While this emotional harangue was in progress, Mitchell leaned over to Saunders and whispered in his ear:

'The old boy's on a sticky wicket, and he knows it. The people will be behind the prince when they hear what's happened. Everybody knows he's been trying to get into space for years.'

'I wish he hadn't chosen *my* ship,' said Saunders. 'And I'm not sure that this doesn't count as mutiny.'

'The heck it does. Mark my words – when this is all over you'll be the only Texan to have the Order of the Garter. Won't that be nice for you?'

'Shush!' said Chambers. The prince was speaking, his

146

words winging back across the abyss that now sundered him from the island he would one day rule.

'I am sorry, Mr. Prime Minister,' he said, 'if I've caused you any alarm. I will return as soon as it is convenient. Someone has to do everything for the first time, and I felt the moment had come for a member of my family to leave Earth. It will be a valuable part of my education, and will make me more fitted to carry out my duty. Good-bye.'

He dropped the microphone and walked over to the observation window – the only spaceward-looking port on the entire ship. Saunders watched him standing there, proud and lonely – but contented now. And as he saw the prince staring out at the stars which he had at last attained, all his annoyance and indignation slowly evaporated.

No one spoke for a long time. Then Prince Henry tore his gaze away from the blinding splendour beyond the port, looked at Captain Saunders, and smiled.

'Where's the galley, Captain?' he asked. 'I may be out of practice, but when I used to go scouting I was the best cook in my patrol.'

Saunders slowly relaxed, then smiled back. The tension seemed to lift from the control room. Mars was still a long way off, but he knew now that this wasn't going to be such a bad trip after all . . .

THE SCIENCE FICTION BOOKS
OF ARTHUR C. CLARKE

THE books are listed in chronological order of publication. The publisher of the first World edition is given, and where this was an American edition this is indicated by (US). Following this, all British editions are listed.

Short stories are indicated by 'collection', Omnibus Editions have a list of contents and these are cross-indexed by the use of In: references. All re-issues of a book under a different title are listed with the original title.

Books published in hardcover are indicated by (hd) while all others are paperbacks. The date for each edition is also given. An asterisk (*) indicates that the edition was in print when this list was compiled in 1973.

BIBLIOGRAPHY

THE SANDS OF MARS
Sidgwick & Jackson (hd), 1951*; Corgi, 1954; Pan, 1964; Sphere, 1969*.
In: *Prelude to Mars*, 1965 (US hd), and *A Second Arthur Clarke Omnibus*, 1968 (hd).

ISLANDS IN THE SKY
Winston (US hd), 1952*; Sidgwick & Jackson (hd), 1952*; Digit, 1964; Puffin (Penguin), 1972*.

CHILDHOOD'S END
Ballantine (US hd/paper), 1953*; Sidgwick & Jackson (hd), 1955*; Science Fiction Book Club (hd), 1955; Pan, 1956*.

In: *Across the Sea of Stars*, 1959 (US hd), and *An Arthur Clarke Omnibus*, 1965 (hd).

AGAINST THE FALL OF NIGHT

Gnome Press (US hd), 1953.

In: *The Lion of Comarre and Against the Fall of Night*, 1968.

Expanded as: *The City and the Stars*, 1956.

EXPEDITION TO EARTH (collection)

Ballantine (US hd/paper), 1953*; Sidgwick & Jackson (hd), 1954*; Corgi, 1959; Pan, 1966; Sphere, 1968*.

PRELUDE TO SPACE

Galaxy S.F., 1951; Sidgwick & Jackson (hd), 1953*; Pan, 1954; New English Library, 1962.

Title change: *Master of Space*.

Lancer (US), 1961.

Title change: *The Space Dreamers*.

Lancer (US), 1969.

EARTHLIGHT

Sidgwick & Jackson (hd), 1954*; Pan, 1957.

In: *Across The Sea of Stars*, 1959, and *A Second Arthur Clarke Omnibus*, 1968.

REACH FOR TOMORROW (collection)

Ballantine (Us hd/paper), 1956*; Gollancz (hd), 1962*; Corgi, 1968*.

THE CITY AND THE STARS

(Expanded and rewritten version of *Against The Fall of Night*)

Harcourt (US), 1956*; Muller (hd), 1959; Corgi, 1957*; Gollancz (hd), 1958*.

In: *From the Ocean, From the Stars*, 1962.

THE DEEP RANGE

Harcourt (US hd), 1957*; Muller (hd), 1957; Science Fiction Book Club (hd), 1960; Gollancz (hd), 1968*; Pan, 1970*.

In: *From the Ocean, From the Stars*, 1962.

TALES FROM THE WHITE HART (collection)
  Ballantine (US), 1957*; Sidgwick & Jackson (hd/paper),
    1972*.
THE OTHER SIDE OF THE SKY (collection)
  Harcourt (US hd), 1958*; Gollancz (hd), 1961*. Science
    Fiction Book Club (hd), 1962; Corgi, 1963*.
  In: *From the Ocean, From the Stars,* 1962.
ACROSS THE SEA OF STARS (collection)
  Harcourt (US), 1959.
  Contains: *Earthlight, Childhood's End* and short stories.
A FALL OF MOONDUST
  Harcourt (US hd), 1961*; Gollancz (hd), 1961*; Science
    Fiction Book Club (hd), 1963; Pan, 1964*.
  In: *A Second Arthur Clarke Omnibus,* 1968.
FROM THE OCEAN, FROM THE STARS (collection)
  Harcourt (US hd), 1962.
  Contains: *The City and the Stars, The Deep Range* and
    The Other Side of the Sky.
TALES OF TEN WORLDS (collection)
  Harcourt (US hd), 1962*; Gollancz (hd), 1963*; Science
    Fiction Book Club (hd), 1964; Pan, 1965; Corgi, 1971*.
DOLPHIN ISLAND
  Winston (US hd), 1963*; Gollancz (hd), 1963*; Dragon
    (Panther), 1968*.
AN ARTHUR CLARKE OMNIBUS (collection)
  Sidgwick & Jackson (hd), 1965.
  Contains: *Childhood's End, Prelude to Space* and *Expe-
    dition to Earth.*
PRELUDE TO MARS (collection)
  Harcourt (US hd), 1965.
  Contains: *Sands of Mars, Prelude to Space* and short
    stories.
TIME PROBE (anthology edited by Arthur Clarke)
  Delacorte (US hd), 1967; Gollancz (hd), 1967.

Nine Billion Names of God (collection)
Harcourt (US hd), 1967.

2001: A Space Odyssey
(Based on the screenplay of the film by Stanley Kubrick and Arthur Clarke.)
New American Library (US hd), 1968*; Hutchinson (hd), 1968*; Arrow, 1968*.

A Second Arthur Clarke Omnibus (collection)
Sidgwick & Jackson (hd), 1968*.
Contains: *Sands of Mars*, *Earthlight* and *A Fall of Moondust*.

The Lion of Comarre and Against the Fall of Night (collection)
Harcourt (US hd), 1968*; Gollancz (hd), 1970*; Corgi, 1972*.

Three for Tomorrow (anthology edited by Arthur Clarke)
Gollancz (hd), 1970*; Sphere, 1972*.

The Lost Worlds of 2001 (collection)
Signet (US), 1972*; Sidgwick & Jackson (hd/paper), 1972*.

The Wind from the Sun (collection)
Harcourt (US hd), 1972*; Gollancz (hd), 1972*.

Of Time and Stars (collection)
Gollancz (hd), 1972*.

Rendezvous with Rama
Gollancz (hd), 1973*; Pan, 1974*.

The Best of Arthur C. Clarke: 1937–1965 (collection)
Sidgwick & Jackson (hd), 1973*; Sphere, 1973*.

A Selection of Classic Short Stories from Sphere

All the above books are edited by Angus Wells

Titles in the Conan Series from Sphere

Exciting Science Fiction/Fantasy written by
Robert E. Howard

CONAN	35p
CONAN THE CONQUEROR	35p
CONAN THE USURPER	35p
CONAN THE WANDERER	35p
CONAN THE WARRIOR	30p
CONAN THE AVENGER	35p
CONAN OF THE ISLES	35p
CONAN THE ADVENTURER	30p
CONAN THE BUCCANEER	40p
CONAN OF CIMMERIA	30p
CONAN THE FREEBOOTER	30p

A Selection of Science Fiction Titles from Sphere

The Simon Rack Series from Sphere

Written by Laurence James

Adventure Fiction from Sphere

A Selection of Warfare Titles from Sphere

A Selection of Occult Titles from Sphere

All Sphere Books are available at your bookshop or
newsagent, or can be ordered from the following address:
Sphere Books, Cash Sales Department,
P.O. Box 11, Falmouth, Cornwall.

Please send cheque or postal order (no currency), and allow
18p for the first book plus 8p per copy for each additional
book ordered up to a maximum charge of 66p in U.K.

Customers in Eire and B.F.P.O. please allow 18p for the first
book plus 8p per copy for the next 6 books, thereafter 3p
per book.

Overseas customers please allow 20p for the first book and
10p per copy for each additional book.